"I know you want me as much as I want you."

Juan's lancing blue eyes dared her to speak the words of denial that trembled on her lips . . . stillborn against the firm compelling pressure of his mouth.

"You're only half alive without me . . . I'm incomplete without you," he muttered as his lips trailed fire down her throat. "Admit it! Tell me what these past few months have been like."

They had been like a never-ending famine, a soul-parching drought, but she was not going to admit it to him.

"Women have other needs beside those of a sexual relationship," she countered.

"Of course," he retorted fiercely. "But you were also made for love . . . for passion. Think back, Josslyn! Remember the times we made love. Don't you remember telling me that you loved me?"

D0191696

ANNABEL MURRAY has pursued many hobbies. She helped found an arts group in Liverpool, England, where she lives with her husband and two daughters. She loves drama: she appeared in many stage productions and went on to write an award-winning historical play. She uses all her experiences—holidays being no exception—to flesh out her characters' backgrounds and create believable settings for her romance novels.

Books by Annabel Murray

HARLEQUIN ROMANCE

These books may be available at your local bookseller.

Don't miss any of our special offers. Write to us at the following address for information on our newest releases.

Harlequin Reader Service
901 Fuhrmann Blvd., P.O. Box 1397, Buffalo, NY 14240
Canadian address: P.O. Box 2800, Postal Station A,
5170 Yonge St., Willowdale, Ont. M2N 6J3

The Plumed Serpent
Annabel Murray

Harlequin Books

TORONTO • NEW YORK • LONDON
AMSTERDAM • PARIS • SYDNEY • HAMBURG
STOCKHOLM • ATHENS • TOKYO • MILAN

Original hardcover edition published in 1986
by Mills & Boon Limited

ISBN 0-373-02782-6

Harlequin Romance first edition August 1986

CHAPTER ONE

'To the new Joss Ransome! A worthy successor to her father!'

'Joss Ransome!' the voices echoed; glasses clinked; the laughter of women tinkled, echoed by that of men in a lower register.

'And don't forget Livings and Son Ltd,' another voice put in. Dutifully the cry went up, 'Livings and Son!'

It had been a typical publishers' party, plenty to eat, plenty to drink; and now it was nearly over. But the acclaim was not; there would be press coverage, media coverage, author tours, and all to launch a book that had been born out of heartache. Josslyn surveyed the gathering with a jaundiced eye. Like many of those present, she had drunk a little too much ... but with the opposite effect. She felt positively depressed.

'Well, darling!' Her mother came towards her, Harry Livings's arm draped familiarly about her slender shoulders. 'Have you enjoyed your party?' She stood on tiptoe to kiss Josslyn's cheek. 'How does it feel to be a success in yet another field? Daddy would have been so proud of you!'

'Would he?' Josslyn asked cynically. 'I wonder!' During the last six months, while her book had been in production, she had been edgy and moody, something her mother and Harry couldn't understand; but then they didn't know the full story of those other months, the three months she'd spent away from home.

'You've done me proud, Joss! Money well invested!' Harry paid his own personal tribute to his protégée, the daughter of one of his most successful, and late lamented, authors. 'Some of your illustrations are

unique, pure gems. Frankly I never expected you to
come back with half the material. Aren't you glad now
that I arranged for you to meet up with de Grijalva?'

If she had been totally sober, Josslyn might not have
been so indiscreet, but now all the weeks of bitterness
rose up in her like bile and, into a sudden silence, she
retorted,

'No, I'm not; Juan de Grijalva is one of the biggest
bastards in the world, and I hope I never have the
misfortune to meet him again!'

'I always hate having to disappoint a lady!' The hard,
assured voice came from just behind her, and with a
startled breath Josslyn swung round to face the
unexpected latecome. Why hadn't Harry told her *he*
would be here?

Afterwards, she maintained that it was the unaccustomed alcohol that had made her head swim and
her legs buckle under her.

Josslyn fought for breath and in an unconscious
gesture her hand went to her breast, where her heart
was behaving most irregularly. Disbelievingly, she
stared up into the familiar bronzed features, with their
frame of gold, met the gaze of lancing blue eyes, saw
them swiftly appraise her tall, splendidly proportioned
body in its white, clinging, Grecian-style gown.

'I must apologise for my lateness.' Juan included
Daphne Ransome and Harry Livings in his apology.
'My flight was delayed.'

'What are *you* doing here?' Josslyn's already husky
voice was a mere croak. She was mortifyingly aware of
the avid stares of those around her. The people who
had been toasting her, lionising her, were just as ready
to seize upon some hint of drama or scandal in her life.
Oh, why had they chosen the precise moment of her
unguarded outburst to fall silent? She tried to shrug off
the strong, tanned hand that had reached out to
support her as she swayed with the shock of seeing Juan
. . . here in London.

'The same as you, I imagine!' That old, familiar smile crinkled the corners of his eyes. 'Celebrating the launch of our book.'

'*My* book!' she said furiously. To Harry's bewilderment, she had refused even to include Juan's name in the acknowledgments. If he thought he could come here and lay some claim to her work, or to her, he could think again. He had, of his own choosing, forfeited all rights.

'Sit down!' It was half command, half suggestion. 'You seem to have been overdoing the celebrations.'

Thank goodness he'd accepted the more obvious explanation of her sudden weakness. She wouldn't want him to have the satisfaction of knowing that it was the sight of him that was making her legs tremble beneath her like this, so that she was glad to sink on to the upholstered window seat, the city outside now just a dark blur, broken by a myriad of lights.

Promptly, disturbingly, Juan joined her. He looked around him, his gaze cynical, as he studied the other guests, most of whom were still stealing covert glances in their direction.

'So you're back in your proper milieu,' he murmured, 'civilisation and all it has to offer.'

She bristled. Was he insinuating that she had not been genuine in her expressed love of the Mexican interior, and her sense of achievement in enduring the primitive conditions to which he had ruthlessly subjected her, without dampening her enthusiasm?

'I'm only in London until I decide where to set my next "Sketchbook",' she returned.

'And who your next "guide" will be?' His voice was suddenly harsh, concentrating her attention more fully upon him. His build had always been lean, his features ascetic, but was he thinner than when she had last seen him?

'There'll be no guide next time,' she said flatly. 'I'll travel alone . . . as I should have done in Mexico.'

'You didn't find my company distasteful all the time,' he mocked, his tone sensually suggestive as he leant nearer, so that the words were for her ear alone, so that his fair beard just brushed the curve of her cheek; the erotic sensation, his words, setting back the clock, so that the crowded room, the buzz of conversation, faded as, unwillingly, golden eyes met dark blue, glittering ones.

'I don't want to be reminded of that,' she whispered painfully, 'and if you had any decency . . .'

'I wouldn't remind you that *you* were the one to break our agreement?'

'Liar! Liar! I . . .'

'I should keep your voice down,' he suggested mildly. 'Your "friends" are watching . . . dying to know what there is between us.'

'Nothing!' she said defiantly, her voice shaky, but still raised an octave. 'There's nothing between us . . . and I'll tell them so.' She jumped to her feet, un- characteristically clumsy in her movements, knocking over a nearby table, the crash of breaking glasses immediately riveting all eyes upon them once more. But before she could open her mouth to make the announcement she threatened, Juan too was on his feet; her elbow was seized in an iron grip, which, to outward appearance, was merely intimate, as he hustled her towards the door.

'Are you staying at this hotel?' he demanded.

'Yes, but . . .'

'Which floor?' He summoned the lift.

'I'm quite capable of finding my own room,' she snapped. 'And besides, I wasn't ready to leave the party. My friends . . .'

'Friends!' he jeered, 'Sycophants, all of them. I know the type. Don't you realise yet? One half of them are here for the free booze and the other half because they might be able to jump on the bandwagon of your success . . . hoping there's something in it somewhere for them . . .'

'Like you!' she interrupted.

His grasp tightened painfully, but he declined to answer her taunt. When the lift arrived, it was crowded, but somehow Juan jammed them both into it.

'Which floor?' he demanded again; his eyes watching her were daring her to defy him. He knew she wouldn't start an argument in front of this crowd of strangers.

'Sixth!' she said briefly, sulkily.

Apprehensively, she watched as, at every floor, the lift became emptier; but at least it meant she could move further away from Juan. Resolutely, she kept her eyes from his face, as if intent upon the illuminated numbers as the lift ascended. The figure six lit up, the door slid open and they were alone in the long, thickly carpeted corridor.

'You needn't come any further,' she told him, as she stopped outside her door.

'You mean you don't want me to come any further,' he rejoined, 'but I intend to do so. I didn't fly thousands of miles just to see you for five minutes.'

'As far as I'm concerned even that is too long!' Still she kept her back to the door, wondering how she could prevent him from gaining access to the room beyond. Once there, she knew, he would have her at a disadvantage.

But even as she sought for some way to be rid of him, he removed the evening bag clasped loosely in her trembling hand and, ignoring her cry of outrage, rifled its contents for her key. Leaning over her shoulder, he deftly inserted the key in the lock; the door swung open and, as it did so, she found herself compelled to move with it. Without undue force, Juan had effected his entry. He closed the door, then he tossed the glittering bag back to her.

'Now . . .' He consulted his wristwatch, satisfaction in his voice. 'If necessary we have all night to talk.'

'You're not staying in my room all night,' she told him, the attractive huskiness of her voice accentuated by stress, but she knew her words were mere bravado. If Juan had decided he was staying, there was no power on earth that could move him. Even if she threatened to scream, it was doubtful that her cries would penetrate the discreet soundproofing of the adjacent rooms, and she knew she wouldn't be allowed to make it to the internal telephone. All she could hope for was that her mother would come up to say good night ... and even that was unlikely. She suspected that Daphne and Harry had plans to go on somewhere after the party, plans that might well involve them until the small hours of next morning.

'Juan, you must see that you can't stay here,' she repeated, hoping he might be more amenable to reason than to hostility.

'No, I don't see.' He moved to sit on the edge of the bed, then looked about him, noting the proportions of the room, its luxurious appointments. 'We've shared smaller spaces than this,' he reminded her, then yawned suddenly. 'God, but I'm tired ... That damned plane. Perhaps it would be a good idea to postpone our talk until later.'

'Yes ... yes ...' she agreed feverishly. 'You ought to get a good night's sleep.'

'Your concern for my welfare touches me,' he said drily, but she rushed on, ignoring the sarcasm.

'I could ring down to reception. I'm sure they'll be able to find you a room. It's not the height of the season.'

'No need.' He yawned again and swung his long legs up on to the bed. 'This will do nicely.' He lay for a moment, watching her through half closed eyes. 'I like the dress!' His voice was purringly seductive, making her heart lurch in the old familiar way. 'If you were to come over here, I could admire it more closely.'

Her stomach clenched against the insidious flattery, she remained safely out of reach. At close quarters, the provocative cut of the Grecian dress, she knew, would be sufficient to have him wide awake and dangerous.

'You look like a goddess, Josslyn, virginal, untouchable ... but you're not, are you?'

Though there was a hint of cruelty in his tone that made her wince inwardly, she remained silent, willing herself to show no reaction. Despite his words, she knew he was barely awake.

'Plenty of room here for both of us,' he murmured insinuatively. Then, as if nothing could hold them open an instant longer, his eyes closed and, after a few moments, she knew he was asleep.

Cautiously, she approached his side of the bed, the side where the telephone was situated; she contemplated summoning assistance, demanding that her unwelcome visitor be ejected; but she dared not reach out to lift the receiver. She'd had startling proof many times of his ability to waken instantly, at the slightest sound. Instead, with unwilling fascination, she found herself staring down at him. It wasn't the first time by a long way that she'd seen Juan de Grijalva asleep, but it was a sight she hadn't expected to witness ever again.

The relaxed position, the strong, lean features with their golden tan, the yellow gold of hair, moustache and beard were so familiar, arousing memories she had believed laid to rest for ever. Now, as she watched his sleeping face, her eyes full of unguarded hunger, she sank down on to the bedside chair and allowed memory to flood back ...

The KLM 747 banked steeply as it crossed the high, beautiful barrier of the mountains that surrounded the former Valley of Anahuac, better known as Mexico City. Then the aeroplane descended through the thick haze of smog ... traffic fumes pouring into the thin air, seven thousand feet above sea level.

Josslyn Ransome stared moodily through the window at a view as obscure and indecisive as her state of mind.

Not that she wasn't excited at the prospect of three
months in this reputedly vivid, vital and colourful
country; she was. It was a long unfulfilled ambition. It
was the circumstances under which this ambition was
being achieved that troubled her, circumstances which
might interfere with something that she valued above
everything else, her independence.

Her mother had been against the trip, but it was not
her mother's objections in themselves which now made
her uneasy, but their outcome.

'Mexico? On your own? Joss, you must be out of
your mind!'

Josslyn's expression as she regarded her diminutive
mother was one of mingled affection and exasperation.

'Mother! I've been travelling around on my own for
five years now, ever since I was twenty. What's so
different about *this* trip?'

'For one thing, on those occasions, you were staying
in nice homes, places where I knew you were safe. You
don't know anything about Mexico ... You don't
know anyone there. Isn't it rather ... rather primitive?
Dangerous? With bandits and ... and things ...?'
Daphne Ransome ended lamely, making her daughter
laugh aloud.

'I think you're a bit out of date, Mum. But in any
case, that's the whole reason ... It's because I *don't*
know anything about Mexico that I want to go. Dad
always said ...' Her voice wobbled uncertainly, as she
thought of her father, his death too recent for her to be
able to speak of him without emotion. 'Dad always said
the next in his series of "Sketchbooks" must be Mexico.
But ... but he didn't have a chance to go there. I want
to do this for him ... as a sort of tribute.'

Both women were silent for a moment, thinking of
Joss Ransome, for whom his daughter had been named
and whose 'Candid Sketchbooks' of the people,
customs and architecture of various countries had
received worldwide acclaim.

'I may never be as good an artist as Daddy,' Josslyn continued after a while, 'but it's something I have to try and do . . . if his publishers agree.'

'I can understand why you want to go,' Daphne Ransome said sadly, 'but I would rather you went on with your nice portraits. I used to worry so dreadfully about your father travelling in such remote places, all alone . . . and he was a man! I'd be even more worried about you.'

'Oh, Mother! Honestly!' Josslyn was laughing, but, nevertheless, she meant every word. 'It's people like you who prolong the myth that women are second-class citizens, that there's some mystique about being male which automatically bestows greater talent, greater capabilities . . .'

'Nonsense!' Daphne Ransome's interruption was quite fierce for Josslyn's usually gentle, feminine mother. 'I hope I'm not *that* old-fashioned. There have been militant women in every age, you know! But Joss . . .' Her voice became pleading. 'Don't become too hard, too unfeminine. If men wanted counterparts of themselves, God wouldn't have created two sexes. I'm sure a lot of those nice men you used to bring home were put off by your independent manner.'

'Deliberately so!' Josslyn said, her frank admission appalling her mother. 'Nice they may have been, but they all wanted the same thing . . . every one of them.'

'Joss!' Now Daphne was shocked. 'You don't mean to say . . .'

'It's all right, Mum. I wasn't referring to sex . . . though that came into it as well.'

'Joss, darling!' Daphne was hesitant now. 'You haven't ever . . .? I mean. I know you young people have different standards these days, but . . .'

'No!' Josslyn said firmly. 'I haven't! My standards are the same as yours. I won't say I haven't been tempted, I'm only human, but . . . oh, I don't know . . . I've always felt it was worth waiting for.' She shrugged.

'I can't say marriage because, quite honestly, I'm not sure that's what I want.'

'Then if those men friends of yours weren't after ... well, what *did* they want? I mean, there *are* only two alternatives, aren't there? An affair ... or marriage?'

'With a couple of exceptions, they all had marriage in mind ... but on their terms. Cosy, suburban, commuter homes, with an obedient little wife cooking, cleaning, pouring the pre-dinner sherry and giving them a quiverful of kids.'

'But, Joss! Don't *you* want children? Not ever?'

'It will probably shock you to the core ... but no, I don't think I do.'

Josslyn thought back over this conversation as she walked briskly across the tarmac towards customs and passport control. Her mother hadn't really understood. Herself quietly, comfortably domesticated, with no particular career skills, Daphne had been quite content to be homemaker for her husband and only daughter, would have welcomed more children if fate had so decreed. Like a hen hatching out a batch of ducklings, she had been alarmed and uncomprehending of the need, shared by husband and daughter, to venture into unfamiliar elements.

Josslyn, as like her father as it was possible for a girl to be, had inherited not only his artistic talent, but also his wanderlust. But, although she disliked her husband's prolonged absences, Daphne would have been equally uncomfortable accompanying him. Hers was not a pioneering spirit.

Growing up, Josslyn had witnessed her mother's ill-concealed apprehension as the time approached when Joss Ransome would take off on another of his sketching trips; she had seen her mother merely existing throughout the months of his absence, going about her chores with a kind of automatic efficiency, as if only part of her were present, the real purpose of her life removed. Daphne had been like this again lately, in the weeks since Joss Ransome's death. Then there had been the mounting excitement in the days preceding her father's return from overseas, the exaltation of the actual moment of reunion, a few succeeding hours in which Josslyn had felt excluded. Not that her parents had meant her to feel left out, but at such times they had been all in all to each other.

As she reached maturity, Josslyn could understand their special relationship ... but not the circumstances which attended it. Though her father was obviously genuinely happy when at home, she knew instinctively, because she was so much his daughter, that when he was away his life was just as enriched and fulfilled, that his love was of his life a thing apart, but Daphne's whole existence.

To herself, Josslyn vowed that she would never submit, as her mother did, to being left, as it were, in cold storage, until her partner chose to return to her. She would share her husband's life, travelling with him if that was what his career entailed, or, if not, she would have an equally absorbing interest to fill their hours apart.

Because she shared and understood her father's wanderlust, it had never occurred to Josslyn that not many men were cast in his mould. She had naturally expected that any man who fell in love with her would be exciting, adventurous. Unconsciously, she now realised, she had been looking for a man who could live up to her father's image, but who would also allow her to be as independent and free a spirit as himself.

It had been an enlightenment and a disappointment to find that most men were quite happy or at least reconciled to toiling a five-day week, from nine till five in stuffy offices, demanding no more of their wives than complacent domesticity. It was ironic, Josslyn reflected, that her mother, whilst adoring her husband as she did, would have been pleased to change him, would, if she could, have kept him chained to dull routine, eradicating the very qualities that made him the man he was. Yet Daphne, because of her adoration, had also been prepared to be what Joss Ransome wanted, had submerged her needs in favour of his.

Josslyn could never imagine tempering *her* lifestyle to dovetail with that of any man, any more than her father had been prepared to be a stereotyped husband. When she'd tried to explain some of this to her mother, Daphne had stated flatly that it was 'different for a woman' and that obviously Josslyn had never really been in love.

Perhaps that was true; but it didn't change anything; somewhere in the world, she argued inwardly, there must be just such another man as her father, with a similar spirit of adventure; if only she could meet him. It didn't even occur to her that if she ever met this ideal man, he too might prefer his wife to keep house, rather than to travel at his side . . . or pursue her own career.

The sun reflected hotly off the tarmac and the glittering glass surfaces of the airport buildings, as Josslyn's queue edged towards the barriers, and it was a relief when, her passport returned, she could reclaim her luggage and look, successfully, for a porter.

At school and afterwards, girlfriends had teased Josslyn about her inches, telling her that she'd never find a man tall enough to match her. But in certain circumstances, Josslyn reflected humorously, her unusual height was very useful in securing attention. It genuinely did not occur to her that her blonde good looks were just as efficacious, that the porter had bypassed two potential customers, just as tall, in order to come to *her* aid.

Before she left England, Harry Livings had given Josslyn a very useful insight into Mexican life and character, one fact being that there were virtually only two classes, the rich and the poor. On the way into

Mexico City from the airport, the delineation between the two was immediately apparent. Around the ultra modern, artistically dazzling sections of the capital, huddled 'spontaneous settlements', vast areas of ramshackle cardboard and tar paper shelters, while somewhat more sturdy were the *barriadas* . . . adobe tenements. The city, though larger than she had expected, was not too different from any other capital: public buildings; orderly brick and chrome business blocks; hotels.

Thank goodness her researches wouldn't involve her in driving around the city, Josslyn thought, as the taxi driver, procured by the admiring, dark-skinned porter, drove rapidly away from the airport, their destination the Hotel San Felipe. Everyone seemed to be in such a hurry and the traffic was a nightmarish free for all. Her own cabbie drove like a demon let loose. Maybe he believed himself to bear a charmed life, for the dashboard of the taxi carried a miniature image of a saint, in front of which a small red lamp was burning. Incongruously, next to this devotional object was a garish, coloured pin up of a girl.

City life was not what Josslyn wanted to portray. Like her father she wanted to record the more remote, the more inaccessible facets of Mexican life: the isolated village; the peasant; the Indian. She even dreamed of discovering some hitherto unknown ruin, though she was realistic enough to know that this last was very unlikely.

The San Felipe was a very expensive hotel, but her mother had insisted that she book in at a quiet, dignified place, in a respectable area. But then, Daphne was not to know, until afterwards, that her daughter planned to travel into the interior, that she intended to stay at the hotel for only a couple of days, which was all it should take her to arrange for the rental of a car, the purchase of camping equipment and, reluctantly, to make the acquaintance of her contact in Mexico City.

Her contact! Josslyn's fine dark brows came together in a sudden frown. That part of her schedule was not at her request; she had only agreed to it to placate her mother's fears for her.

The hotel was large, the main part of it being nine storeys high. Some of the rooms faced the mountains, offering an incomparable view. But, her thoughts turned inward, Josslyn stared unseeingly, unappreciatively. She was tired ... the journey; the unaccustomed altitude. It was this altitude, already catching up with her, as much as a strong disinclination for her errand, which made her decide to postpone the irritating necessity of contacting Juan de Grijalva until the next day.

Juan de Grijalva! Josslyn could just imagine him! He would be a fat, swarthy, mustachioed little man, with pudgy hands, an opinionated manner and an acquisitive gleam in his eye, as befitted a dealer in antiquities. His high-class establishment, she'd been given to understand, was in the Zona Rosa, one of the city's most elegant sections.

'I don't *need* a contact,' she'd protested vigorously, when she and her mother had visited the London office of Joss Ransome's publisher.

Over the years of his long association with Joss, Harry Livings had also become a family friend. In fact, Josslyn suspected that the short, dumpy, rather ugly man was in love with her mother; and she pitied him; for even when Daphne's grief had faded, Josslyn doubted he would ever stand a chance against the memory of her tall, vividly handsome father.

Now Harry reasoned with her ... for Daphne's sake, he said.

'Contact Senor de Grijalva, please, Joss, if only to set your mother's mind at rest. And besides, you may very well be glad of his help and influence on your own account. It *is* still possible for foreigners to run into trouble in Mexico. There's still a certain amount of hostility and mistrust towards outsiders, even though it's many centuries since they were a conquered race.'

'One woman with a sketchbook and a camera scarcely represents an invasion,' Josslyn pointed out.

'No, but on the other hand, the Mexican doesn't accord women, especially foreign women, the same respect and equality as his European counterpart.'

'You're saying they're a load of male chauvinist pigs?' Unperturbed, Josslyn smiled. 'There are plenty of them in this country, you know, and I'm not an inexperienced teenager.'

'I would say that the Mexican is the original chauvinist pig, that he invented the term "machismo". His womenfolk expect and accept domination.'

'And yet you're asking me to make contact with one of them, rely on him if necessary? A bit illogical, isn't it?'

'Ah well!' Harry Livings demurred. 'Juan de Grijalva is ... different. He's also by way of being a personal friend of mine. Anyone recommended to him by me is sure of a courteous welcome, respectful treatment and considerable help.' He darted a look at Daphne Ransome, which seemed to convey some special message of reassurance, for Josslyn sensed a relaxation of her mother's tension. Instantly she was suspicious. What were these two plotting? Harry, she knew, only had her best interests at heart and she was grateful to him for that. But she had no wish to be represented to this de Grijalva as a helpless, clinging female in need of perpetual guidance and protection.

'I won't tolerate any interference,' she warned.

'Now, Joss!' Harry's chubby features were the picture of injured innocence. 'Did I mention interference? Help is what I said and help is what I meant.'

Reluctantly, Josslyn accepted his reassurance, though some sixth sense told her that her mother and Harry were keeping something back. It was annoying that Daphne still regarded her as a child; but that, she understood, was a common maternal syndrome. But even Harry, who was no relation, had been dubious when she'd suggested she continue her father's work.

'The "Candid Sketchbooks" have been very successful and I won't deny they've netted our firm a nice little profit. But don't do this because you feel you have to worry about your mother's finances. The royalties, together with your father's investments, will give her a comfortable yearly income for the rest of her life.'

'It's not just the money,' Josslyn assured him. 'It's just something I have to do, for Dad. There were so many more countries he wanted to include in the series. And—I don't know if you can understand this—in a way, I want to *prove* myself . . . to prove that women can compete in the same field.'

'Yes. I understand. You're Joss's daughter through and through and he'd be proud of your motives. But— forgive me—I know you're talented, but in a different genre. *Can* you produce the same mood, the same atmosphere as your father? And then you are an unknown and, however determined you are, it *is* more difficult for a woman to cope with the physical challenges of countries less civilised than our own, extremes of climate, the risks implied just by the very fact that you *are* female . . . You . . . you know what I mean?'

Yes, she knew what Harry was trying to say in his floundering, rather old-fashioned way. But these outmoded conceptions of womanhood were just what she wanted to confound. Nevertheless, he was weakening. She sensed that and she leant forward eagerly; her words came quickly, willing him to agree.

'Harry, if I promise to take care . . . if I *can* reproduce my father's style, and I think I can, need anyone know? You could be publishing posthumous work . . .' She stopped as he slowly shook his head.

'No, Joss! Oh, I know you intend it as a tribute to your father, but he wouldn't have seen it that way. He wouldn't have wanted you to stifle your own artistic style, to slavishly imitate his . . .'

Her shoulders slumped.

'Then you won't back me?'

'Yes, but as yourself. This once. And if things work out . . . Well, there'll be more "Sketchbooks", but they'll be by Josslyn Ransome, not Joss.'

Harry was a darling, Josslyn thought, remembering these words as she set out next day to visit Señor de Grijalva's emporium. Harry was much more the sort of man her mother should have married. But thank goodness she didn't, she thought, or I wouldn't be *me*! Suddenly she was filled with a sense of glorious elation, of well-being. It was good to be alive, soon to be setting off on an exciting new enterprise. This must be how her father had felt at the beginning of each expedition. She'd experienced this euphoria before, in a milder way. Her own travels had taken her to many interesting places, but interesting in a different sense. The challenge then had been in what she was to do, rather than in the setting itself.

Josslyn might be an unknown, as Harry had said, in the world of publishing, but not in the art world. An accomplished portrait painter, she had been commissioned many times to portray the famous, the wealthy of other countries besides her own. As she had reminded her mother, she was accustomed to travelling alone, even if only to the civilised comfort of her subjects' homes. But this would be real adventure.

It had taken her a while to decide what to wear for her visit to Juan de Grijalva. Although she would not admit the necessity for it, she had an uneasy feeling that Harry expected her to make a certain impression on the Señor. But what sort of impression? Was she supposed to charm him to ensure his goodwill or to impress him with her capability? How would she appear to a complete stranger?

She was not much given to studying her own appearance, but in this case ... The hotel bedroom's cheval-glass gave her a full length view. Tall ... five foot eight in stockinged feet. Her thick fair hair in a short, expensively casual cut, made a sleek silver cap about her head. From high cheekbones, her face curved down to a round, determined chin. Wide-spaced, sooty-lashed eyes of an unusual clear gold lent a hint of the unusual to her appearance. Her full lips formed a natural pout, but could form into stubborn lines if necessary ... and they did now. To hell with it, she decided. It didn't matter two hoots to her what he thought of her appearance. They were going to meet, exchange meaningless courtesies, arrange for him to receive any important mail from home, forward her letters to her mother ... and that would be that.

Most of the outfits she had brought with her were trouser suits, geared towards travelling and camping in the interior, and she settled for one of these, in a workmanlike shade of khaki. Her vivid complexion needed no more than a moisturiser and, with the minimum of eyeshadow and a touch of lipstick, she was satisfied.

The city was an easy place in which to get lost. Streets changed names as they crossed from one neighbourhood to another. Several times she had to make use of her limited knowledge of Spanish to enquire the way. Many of the thoroughfares were curves or diagonals and it was difficult to hurry on the crowded footpaths. Demonic when behind the wheel of a car, the pedestrian Mexican sauntered, stopped to window shop, to gossip ... But finally Josslyn reached the Zona Rosa.

It seemed to be the 'with-it' part of the city: pavement cafés with gay umbrellas; loud discothèques; chic boutiques. Fascinated, she found *herself* window shopping, perhaps deliberately delaying the moment when she must 'report' to Senor de Grijalva, for that was how it felt to her. But she was genuinely attracted too, to the exclusive jewellers, the leather and craft shops; studios where painters painted and models modelled; and, inevitably, there were the dealers, selling everything from Mexican curios to eighteenth-century antiques; and here was the address she had been told to look for: Quetzalcoatl, Ave Acapulco 169.

Señor de Grijalva's premises were all that she had expected . . . and more. His was not the type of antiques shop that Josslyn delighted to explore . . . a crowded hugger-mugger treasure trove of unexpected delights. This was real class: a tastefully draped window, containing only a few items. The price of each one, she guessed, would be astronomical . . . enough probably, she found herself brooding, to feed and clothe several poor Mexican families for a year.

Josslyn had never been a campaigner for human rights; she had, like every other thinking person, deplored the existence of the underprivileged of any race, but, apart from contributing to Third World appeals, she had always been too much absorbed in her career to take an active interest. Perhaps, she thought, it was because, unreasonably, she admitted, she already felt an antipathy towards Juan de Grijalva that she found herself resenting the opulence of his showrooms, his obvious affluence. She wondered how on earth Harry Livings had made his acquaintance for, though wealthy, the publisher's lifestyle was one of surprising simplicity and she knew he, too, donated liberally to various charities.

But she could procrastinate no longer. The sooner this meeting was over, the sooner she could be about the real purpose of her presence in Mexico. She pushed open the heavy door and stepped into hushed, carpeted, air-conditioned quiet, a sharp contrast to the heat and hubbub of the street outside. Showcases, plate glassed and chrome edged, each illuminated by an individual pool of light, displayed more wares.

At once, a stout, formally suited, dark skinned man stepped out of the shadows at the rear of the shop. Could this be the man she had come to see? He fitted her preconceived image, but would the proprietor himself serve a casual customer?

'*Buenos días, Señorita! Que desea usted?*'

'*No hablo español,*' she told him, then, 'Señor de Grijalva?' She hoped he spoke English. Her knowledge of Spanish was very limited indeed, and apart from that she knew Mexican Spanish varied quite considerably from that spoken in Spain.

'The Señor is busy ... very busy,' the stout man informed her sternly. 'I am here to assist you.'

'But it's Señor de Grijalva I've come to see.' Josslyn could be firm too. 'He is expecting me.'

'Ah ...' At once the man was all apologies, all smiles ... two perfect rows of white teeth in the soft copper complexion. 'In that case ...' Somewhere out of sight he must have touched an unseen bell, for she heard its distant reverberations.

Tapping an impatient, sandalled foot, Josslyn looked towards the rear of the shop, from which Juan de Grijalva might be expected to appear. She felt she was wasting time. All she wanted to do was to introduce herself and then, having fulfilled her obligation to Harry, and thus to her mother, set about her preparations for her tour.

But it was not a man who emerged; it was a daintily built mestizo girl, her delicate features—skin a shade deeper than magnolia, over mongol cheekbones—framed by long swinging black hair, making her outstandingly beautiful.

'*Si?* Can I help you?' she enquired. 'Benito?' She turned to the assistant. '*Que pasa?*'

'The Señorita wishes to see the Señor. She is expected.'

'Oh?' The girl assessed Josslyn. 'You have the appointment? I do not recall . . .'

'I don't need an appointment . . .' Josslyn began.

'But *si* . . . all peoples need appointment. Señor de Grijalva is a very busy man.'

'So everyone keeps telling me!' Josslyn snapped, her patience finally exhausted. She raised her voice, hoping that it would carry to the man who, presumably, inhabited the quarters from which the girl had appeared. 'And I am a very busy woman. I don't have an appointment, because I was told Señor de Grijalva would see me at any time. I'm Joss Ransome.'

The dark eyebrows rose in an arc of incredulity.

'You? You are Joss Ransome? But he is a man . . .'

'Was,' Josslyn said, with the old familiar feeling of pain. 'Joss Ransome was my father. I'm named for him,' she explained impatiently.

'Oh, I see . . .' The almond-shaped, Latin eyes were suddenly hostile, red lips pursed tightly. An expression crossed the other girl's face, which Josslyn could only interpret as one of displeasure. '*Entiendo* . . . I understand. Juan did not explain. I think now I see why . . .'

'Look, can I see him or not?' Josslyn interrupted. 'Because it doesn't matter a damn to me. I only promised to look him up, because . . .'

'Manuela?' At that moment she herself was interrupted by a distant voice which, apart from a very slight intonation, spoke impeccable English. 'Manuela, what the devil are you doing out there? You know I want to finish this inventory today . . .' The volume of the voice grew as its author approached, then a man stepped out into the showroom, ducking his head as he did so. As he stood erect once more, his face sharply illuminated by one of the bright pools of light, Josslyn drew in a startled and, she hoped afterwards, inaudible breath that was almost one of recognition. Her heart began to thud heavily, her blood to tingle. She had heard of instant sexual chemistry, but she had never before experienced . . . and *this* was de Grijalva?

The mestizo girl turned, her sullen expression transformed.

'Júan, *querido*! This woman insists she see you . . . Then,' accusingly, 'she say her name Joss Ransome?'

'Ah . . .' At once the lean, intelligent face was alert. 'Yes, Harry's protégée!'

'You did not say to me Joss Ransome is a woman . . .'

'Didn't I?' He sounded surprised, but Josslyn immediately suspected his air of innocence. 'It must have slipped my mind.' His eyes were intent, comprehensively assessing as he moved forward, hand extended. 'Miss Ransome? Juan de Grijalva, at your service.' The last sounded mocking, a mere form of politeness . . . and Josslyn thought she knew why. This man would never be at anyone's service. This was not the plump, swarthy, ingratiating Mexican tradesman of her imagination. He had the carriage, the features, of the proud hidalgos who must have been his distant forebears, the Spanish conquerors of Mexico; and his skin colouring was no deeper than that of a respectable Riviera tan. But even more amazing was the colour of his hair, moustache and beard . . . a ripe, shining gold that rivalled a summer cornfield. The contrast between skin and hair was eye-catching. He was formally suited in lightweight cream; his pale blue shirt set off a neatly knotted, darker blue tie. Usually fair men didn't appeal to her, but . . .

Josslyn placed her fingers in his, her voice huskily uncertain as she muttered some acknowledgment, she wasn't sure what; some conventional words, which she hoped didn't betray the mental disorder into which his appearance had thrown her. She was tall for a woman, but he towered over her. His hand was hard and strong, as was his grasp; hard and calloused. Hands that worked with fragile antiques? She had always believed

that a man's handshake characterised his personality. If
this was so, Juan de Grijalva's character was a tough
and forceful one. If she hadn't been a stranger to such a
weak emotion, she would have said that it was fear that
suddenly constricted her throat, clenched her stomach
muscles. But there was no reason why she should fear
such a casual acquaintance. She had made her presence
in Mexico known to him and in a few moments she
would leave, as free and independent as upon her
arrival. Pointedly, she withdrew the hand which it
seemed to her he had held overlong, though it was only
a conventional matter of seconds.

'You'd better come through to my office. Manuela,
make us some coffee, will you?'

Bemusedly, Josslyn followed him, struggling as she
did so to readjust her ideas. He motioned her to a chair,
seating himself behind his desk, carefully, methodically,
moving piles of papers to one side; Josslyn took the
opportunity of the few brief seconds to study him
further. Tall, lean, but well built, his face, too, was long
and lean, ascetic almost to the point of gauntness,
relieved only by the soft corn silk of his facial hair; his
nose classically aquiline. His mouth, though well
shaped, had stern, no-nonsense lines to it. His eyes, she
realised, were blue, but so dark that they seemed almost
black and they were, in their turn, subjecting her to a
steady surveillance. Then he smiled, a smile which had
imperceptible beginnings until it lit his whole face,
softening its austere planes, crinkling the skin at the
corners of his eyes. He nodded his head, as if satisfied
about something.

'Yes, you are Joss's daughter. He spoke much of you.
You're like him.'

'You *knew* my father?' Josslyn's golden eyes widened
with an interest she had not expected to feel for this
man, with a need to know what he could tell her of the
other side of her father's life. He inclined his blond
head.

'I had the privilege of working with him twice ... at Tara, and at San Augustin.'

'Working with him?' Josslyn remembered vividly, as she did all her father's 'Sketchbooks', the one on Colombia, which had included the large stone statues of San Augustin ... many of them as much as thirteen feet tall, with terrifying human faces, teeth like cats; some apparently feeding on the children they held. And Tara? 'Do you mean Tara in County Meath?' she asked doubtfully.

'Yes, of course.' He said it as if wondering why there should be any question. 'My father was of Spanish descent, but my mother is Irish, though I was born here in Mexico. I wanted to visit my mother's home ... that was where I first met your father, sketching the earthworks and burial mounds. We fell into conversation and I found that his interests included ancient civilisations and customs, that he planned to go to South America. So I offered to guide him around Colombia and in particular San Augustin. We had much in common and we had intended to make another expedition together ... to Olduvai Gorge, in the Serengeti. But then, sadly, I heard of his death. He never mentioned my name to you?'

'Never,' Josslyn shook her head. 'So you're not *just* an antique dealer?' Disarmed by the fact that Juan de Grijalva had known her father, she forgot her intention that this meeting should be a brief one. This man could tell her about a side of Joss Ransome's life which had been largely unknown to his family.

'Antique dealer?' He shrugged. 'Yes, in part. Also archaeologist, student of human life, explorer ... as much as one *can* explore these days. There's not much of the world left to discover, worse luck!'

'Your English is very good, but then, you said your mother's Irish?'

'Many educated Mexicans speak good English,' he said with a touch of hauteur. 'But it is true that having an English-speaking mother helped. Also I was at your Cambridge University.' He became brisk. 'But enough of me. We're wasting time. There will be plenty of opportunity to learn about each other during our travels.'

'*Our* travels?' Startled out of her sense of false security, Joss's golden eyes widened with apprehension.

'Naturally I shall accompany you.'

'Oh ... oh no. I planned this as a solo enterprise. I don't need a wet nurse.' Or any distractions, she added mentally, sane enough to know that Juan de Grijalva could prove a distracting influence. It was ridiculous that she could react so strongly to a complete stranger, a reaction half attraction, half antagonism.

'Are you implying that your father did?' And, before she could indignantly refute his suggestion, 'Your father welcomed my company; but it was Harry Livings's suggestion, not my idea that, as with your father, we should travel together, since our interests overlap in the same way.'

'Look, Señor de Grijalva, I'm sure you mean well, but I'm not stupid. I know this is a put up job, that it's Harry's idea of protecting me ... just to keep my mother happy. But it doesn't mean I have to accept it and there's no earthly reason why you should leave your business just to explore your own country. You probably know it inside out already.'

'This is what I am telling him!' Unseen, the dainty Manuela had entered via a curtained alcove, with the coffee. With a toss of her dark head, she continued, '*I* should not need a man at my beck and call for so simple a task as to travel this country.'

'No, Manuela!' Juan interjected before Josslyn could reply. 'But then this is *your* country. You have no need to fear it ...'

'Even if I were afraid, I should scorn to show it!' the mestizo girl persisted. 'Me, I have courage, the courage of your *abuelita*, your grandmother. She has said it.'

'No one is doubting *your* courage, Manuela.' Juan spoke patiently. 'But Miss Ransome's case *is* rather different!'

And what was that supposed to mean? Josslyn wondered indignantly. Just give her a chance to show these arrogant Mexicans what British women were made of! What she was made of!

'Well, it is not fair to your family or your friends that you disappear for months on end. That is bad enough, but that you hold the hand of this woman ...' That Manuela counted herself in the latter category of friend, that she implied something deeper than friendship, was obvious to Josslyn; and she wondered fleetingly just where Manuela did fit into Juan de Grijalva's life ... assistant? secretary? girlfriend?'

'That is enough, Manuela!' Juan rebuked. 'You are discourteous. My family understand my need to travel ... and those who wish to remain my friends must do likewise.'

Though, in the circumstances, the rebuke was gentle enough, Juan's accompanying smile lessening its severity, the mestizo girl seemed to contemplate making a retort. Then she obviously thought better of it. But there was a decided flounce to her hips as she banged out of the office.

'Now.' Again Juan was businesslike. 'You'll need a few days to get acclimatised, of course, then your itinerary must be planned.'

'Acclimatised?' She stared at him. 'I want to get started right away. My publisher is paying my expenses ... but to work, not to lounge around Mexico City. And as for an itinerary, I don't intend to have one. I'm going to hire a car and some camping equipment and just wander as the mood takes me ...' Then, positively, '*Alone!*'

But he was shaking his golden head.

'I can't allow that, and ...' raising his hand as she opened her mouth to protest further, 'don't think I can't prevent it. And if you force my hand, I will. Being of some repute, I wield sufficient influence. One word from me and your tourist card would be rescinded ... and remember, in Mexico, our laws are different. Here you are guilty until proved innocent. I would rather not have to accuse you of some misdemeanour.'

How could she ever have found this man attractive? Outraged, Josslyn leapt up, the impulsive act sending her coffee flying, staining the light coloured carpet and also, to her fury, her khaki trouser suit.

'That ... that's blackmail and you're ... despicable! And you dare to call yourself a friend of my father!' Her silver head lifted proudly. 'He'd disown your acquaintance!'

'My dear girl ...' He rounded the desk, proferring his handkerchief to mop at the spreading stain. 'I certainly wouldn't be a worthy friend of your father if I allowed you to go careering around on your own. Tell me honestly ... are you used to primitive living conditions? Admit you know nothing of Mexican customs; you could be flouting them at every step. You speak scarcely any Spanish ... and how do you imagine you're going to communicate with the remote peoples I imagine you intend to visit? Many of them speak only their own dialects.'

'Which *you* of course speak like a native!' she snapped, brushing aside his helpful hand, the touch of which had made her tremble like an impressionable teenager.

'Of course! Come Josslyn, be reasonable. You surely don't want your research to be confined to Mexico City itself ... to the museums, which is what withdrawal of your tourist card could mean. Not much of a follow up to your father's work? Surely you'd rather we reached an amicable agreement?'

Josslyn was in no mood for amity and she bitterly resented this attempt to curtail her independence; resented his familiarity ... and the fact that, despite all this, his proximity could make her insides quiver.

'No, I wouldn't. I'd rather be allowed to please myself . . . and who said you could use my first name?' she enquired haughtily.

'My apologies, Señorita Ransome!' He gave a perfectly executed punctilious bow, much as his aristocratic ancestors might have done, a bow which also contrived to be mocking. 'But I think I will call you Josslyn, *con su permiso*? And in return, you will call me Juan.'

Her reaction to his slow smile, unexpectedly charming, was swiftly quelled as she recalled the forerunner to this exchange. He needn't think he could win her over that easily.

'You're the most irritatingly impossible man I've ever encountered,' she told him stiffly.

'It's fortunate for you,' he said wryly, 'that I'm not a typical product of my country. No Mexicano permits a woman to speak to him so. It would offend his machismo, another good reason why you should not go blundering round alone.'

'Oh, I was warned about that,' Josslyn tossed her head, 'but it doesn't seem to me that there's anything all that special about Mexicans. Men everywhere are all alike . . . and you're just typical, part Mexican or not.'

'And you, Josslyn,' he asked with an affectation of deep interest, 'are you a typical woman of your country?'

Was she? Suddenly she realised she had no standards by which to measure herself. Her career had left her little time for intimate female relationships.

Juan de Grijalva was looking at her in a way, which, while not exactly offensive, was arousing once more those unexpected sensual tinglings in her blood.

'You've been to England,' she reminded him hastily. 'Don't *you* know? You must have met plenty of English girls.

'Yes. I confess I didn't find any particular difference. Like all women, they're emotionally dependent. They tend to cling, to try and tie a man down, curtail his freedom. In fact, at twenty-five, I'm only surprised that *you* haven't settled down yet, tamed some poor man to the collar and lead.' Again, that devastating smile.

'I take it then that you're not tied down,' she said waspishly. Why should his disparaging remark annoy her so much, when she shared his sentiments about possessiveness? Probably because he knew her age ... Harry again? ... and thought she'd been left on the shelf, instead of choosing to be free.

'I'm not married, no,' he drawled. 'That *was* what you were trying to find out?'

She shrugged, piqued again that he should think his marital status of any consequence to her. Did he think she was hanging out for a husband? Had he observed her startled reactions to him? The fear that she might have revealed the way in which he had disrupted her normal self-possession made her sharp.

'I'm not really interested in anything about you. It just seemed to me that a man who was married would scarcely be offering to escort another woman into the interior.'

'Even if I had been fool enough to allow some woman to trap me into marriage, I should expect my wife to trust me absolutely ... whatever the sex of the traveller I accompanied. But, if you're enquiring, obliquely, about your own risk in accepting my company, you needn't worry. I don't go in for emotional involvements. I prefer to remain a free agent ... and the women friends I have accept this. If you decide to be sensible and accept my help, I can assure you our relationship will be that of colleagues ... purely professional.'

No involvements ... purely professional. That was OK by Josslyn, she assured herself. She didn't want Juan de Grijalva in her life in any capacity. She couldn't know that it wouldn't turn out quite like that; his acquaintance was to be forced upon her ... with all its attendant complications.

CHAPTER TWO

IT was infuriating to be delayed. Inclined to be impulsive and headstrong, once she had decided upon a project, Jossyln was all for immediacy of action; and the delays Juan de Grijalva imposed upon her were doubly aggravating, since she considered them to be totally unnecessary. Insistent upon an acclimatisation period, he also admitted that the delay was partly due to the impossibility of him leaving the city just at present.

'One or two business deals require my personal attention.'

Yet he still refused to let her start out alone, still held over her head the threat of her tourist card being rescinded . . . for her own good, he told her. 'I hate wasting time!' she told him, fury darkening the gold of her eyes to molten copper. 'And other people's money.'

'As to that, there's no reason why a few days' delay should cost you time, or Harry Livings his money. You intended to give up your hotel room in any case? Good! Do so! My hospitality is at your disposal . . . and I may have a free hour or two . . .' He ignored the derisive, unappreciative noise she made. 'There's a lot of useful research you can be doing locally, in the museums and . . .'

'I didn't come here to tramp round dusty old museums,' she protested, 'I want to represent things as they are . . . in their natural settings, not behind plate glass.'

'And how will you identify these "things" unless you know what you're looking for?' he enquired ironically. 'A carving or an artefact disguised by dirt, altered by weathering, is totally unrecognisable, unless you "get your eye in" by looking at restored examples.'

Much as she wanted to argue, for in spite of his sexual magnetism, he was capable of angering her more than any other man ... any other person ... she had ever met, she could not do so. Common sense told her, unwillingly, that he was right. She *did* need to prime her untutored eye. But as to accepting his hospitality? She would soon be seeing more than enough of him for her own peace of mind.

'I can always move to a cheaper hotel and ...'

'Which may well be in an unsalubrious area. I think not. My house is your house ... and you'll be well chaperoned: my mother; my grandmother; and Manuela of course.'

'Chaperoned? Since I'm to travel with you, without ...'

'Even then you need have no fear. I've already made my feelings quite clear on that point ... remember? Remember too that *I* didn't invite you to come to Mexico. I'm merely obliging an old friend. My interest in you is ... and will remain ... totally a business one.'

Which wasn't exactly flattering, Josslyn supposed, but it was reassuring and she found that she needed that sense of reassurance. It wasn't only that she was attracted to Juan de Grijalva, that in appearance he did rather resemble the ideal man of her imaginings, but with his forceful aura of masculinity, his arrogance, she had an idea that if he set out to sweep a woman off her feet, he might be difficult to resist ... and that sort of complication she could do without, especially as there was no chance of it leading to happiness. As she'd told her mother, she was only human, a statement which had been tellingly proven in the last hour or so.

Above Mexico City, the mountain road rose in a wide curve, up to a point where houses had finally ceased to surge on to the foothills, meeting the pine forests. This evidently was the city's most fashionable and expensive residential suburb, its villas and mansions citadels of luxury. Beyond wide, neat grass verges, the buildings stood, enclosed by high walls and surrounded by magnificent gardens. Some were all streamlined simplicity; others, like Juan's house, an elaboration of stone and wrought iron around doors and windows, in Spanish feudal style. The white walls were aglow with wine-coloured bougainvillaea, the whole framed by the blue haze of jacaranda trees. The villa was built, hacienda style, around four sides of a tree-grown, flower-filled terrace, on to which opened the ground floor rooms. Stone balconies ran around the upper floor, supporting wrought iron railings.

Inside the heavy wooden main door, sparkling white walls were repeated, contrasting with dark beams and red tiles. The architecture mingled the best of the Spanish style with more modern designs, The high-ceilinged living room consisted of an enormous furnished area, surrounding an indoor pool. There were plants everywhere and the louvred ceiling was open, admitting sunlight. But for the furniture, Josslyn would have thought herself to be in an enormous conservatory. Here, she was introduced to Bridget de Grijalva and after a few minutes, Juan left the two women alone to get acquainted.

Though she might have married a Spanish Mexican and lived in exotic conditions, Bridie O'Hara, as she had once been, had retained her own individuality. Of medium height, vivacious, tending towards plumpness, simply dressed for all the wealth surrounding her, her brogue undiluted even by years spent among Spanish speaking peoples, Bridget might never have left her native land. She accorded Josslyn a warm welcome, delighted to see a fellow European, and was not, as Josslyn had feared she might be, affronted at her son's intention to travel into the interior with an un-chaperoned woman.

'Bless us! You'll be safe enough with Juan. I only wish he *were* likely to become interested in you,' was her startling comment, after Josslyn had nervously explained the total innocence of their proposed association. 'Here's me with one foot in the grave and not a sign of any grandchildren. Himself always saying he'll not be tied down by *any* woman. Even my mother-in-law can't move him. She . . .' And here Josslyn had the idea that Bridget most certainly did not approve. 'She has a wife in mind for him . . . a girl who comes of a race whose women are taught to be submissive, to accept that a man is a free agent.'

'Manuela?' Josslyn guessed.

'Yes! Oh! Of course, you've met her.'

Privately, Josslyn thought that, from what she'd seen of the mestizo girl, Manuela had displayed decidedly the possessive tendencies that Juan deplored in a woman, but it was not her business to comment.

'I suppose you have a boyfriend waiting for you back home?' Bridget asked. 'No?' in surprise, as Josslyn shook her head. 'Oh dear . . .' She sounded distressed, 'You will take care? I wouldn't like you to get . . . hurt.'

'Hurt?'

'Yes! Do you . . . what do you think of my son? I mean . . . oh, I know I shouldn't say this about my own flesh and blood, but there's something about him. He seems to have the power to draw the heart out of a woman entirely. I've seen it happen so many times. 'Tis like watching moths burn their wings at a candle . . . and not a flicker of interest from him. It's afraid I am, if your heart's not already given, you'll . . .'

'Don't worry, Bridie.' The older woman had asked to be addressed informally.. 'I've met plenty of attractive men . . . and survived. I don't think I can be very susceptible. Like your son, I enjoy my freedom too much.' But had she ever met a man quite like Juan de Grijalva? she wondered, with a shiver of premonition that belied her confident statement.

Later, over lunch, Bridget heartily endorsed her son's

invitation to Josslyn to stay at the villa for several days, while she became acclimatised.

''Twill be an unusual experience for me to have a visitor that he doesn't snatch from under my nose only hours after they arrive. So while she's staying here, I'll thank you, Juan, not to monopolise Josslyn's time.'

Knowing Juan's distaste for feminine restraints, Josslyn wondered how he would react to this remark, an example of domestic tyranny, and she was considerably surprised when he merely laughed.

'*Si, madre mia* ... But don't forget,' he warned, 'Josslyn is here to work. Her publishers aren't paying her to socialise, nor to indulge the whims of a garrulous Irish biddy.'

Which was rich, considering how *he* was delaying her, considering *his* whims.

'Irish biddy is it?' his mother demanded indignantly. 'To be sure, if they weren't two feet above my head, I'd box your ears for you!'

Garrulous certainly described Bridget de Grijalva. Throughout the next few hours, she scarcely paused to draw breath; and most of her talk concerned her son, of whom she was obviously immensely proud, but whom, just as obviously, she infrequently saw.

One wing of the villa, she told Josslyn, housed Bridget's mother-in-law, Doña Albina de Grijalva-Lopez, now very aged and infirm, with whom Juan was spending his evening.

'She, too, welcomes Juan's rare visits ... so tonight she shall have her grandson to herself, since I have you. We will have to call upon "La Abuelita", as Juan calls her, but not until tomorrow. I hope this will not be your only visit to us?"

'I'd like to come again ... if there's time. It depends how my work goes.' This was not just politeness on Josslyn's part. Since meeting Bridget, she was beginning to feel that she might actually enjoy her enforced stay at Juan's home. She had liked Bridget immediately and found herself looking forward, too, to meeting the elderly Señora. Doña Albina, she supposed, would be very much the *grande dame* and matriarch of the family and she wondered, with the familiar, intuitive itch of her fingers . . . an instinct which seldom failed her . . . whether there might not be a subject there for a portrait. Perhaps when she knew the family a little better, she might broach the subject.

'Manuela is Doña Albina's companion . . . and the girl she would like Juan to marry. My mother-in-law makes a great favourite of her.' Bridget frowned. 'And I wish she wouldn't. The girl's getting impertinent. When she's not here, she's supposed to help Juan at the shop. But that's just a ploy. She's no use to him. She's no head for business at all.' Bridget chattered on. 'Juan does a lot of good work among the indigenous tribes. He doesn't want to see their cultures destroyed by civilisation. That's another reason why Manuela shouldn't be here. But Doña Albina insisted and she's educated the girl above her own people, the Olmecs. If she'd been left where she was, she might have been married now, according to their own rites. But Juan never goes against his grandmother's wishes. Somehow he seems reluctant to thwart her.'

However powerful the influence of this unknown matriarch, Josslyn doubted that Juan would marry to please anyone except himself, that he would ever provide poor Bridget with the grandchildren she longed for. *Poor* Bridget? She caught herself up on the thought. Wasn't her own mother in exactly the same position, always talking wistfully of the day when Josslyn would make *her* a grandmother? Yet she, Josslyn, felt exactly as Juan did . . . a reluctance to form permanent ties. But she didn't condemn her own views; she was merely living her life as she wished to do, as she had a right to do. So which was the correct view of the situation? This enigma still unsolved, she fell asleep.

* * *

The de Grijalvas might be wealthy, their surroundings palatial, but their meals were simple. Juan, Josslyn noticed when she came down to breakfast next morning, was eating fried eggs, beans and tortillas. Dismayed, she wondered if she would be able to cope with the highly spiced food and the coffee, which, she had already discovered, Mexicans liked 'as black as night, hot as hell and sweet as love'. But Bridget came to her rescue.

'I thought you'd be liking a simple breakfast? Myself, even after all my years in Mexico, I keep to a continental breakfast ... hot rolls and a "decent" cup of coffee ... a taste I acquired when I was working my way around Europe.'

'When was this?' Josslyn enquired curiously.

'Oh, in my teens. I couldn't abide to think of all the world God had made and myself living in only a small portion of it. I thought I'd always be footloose and fancy free ... and I was twenty-six before I finally came to Mexico and met Juan's father.'

So *that* was where Juan got his wanderlust ... from his mother!

'And you didn't mind giving up your travels? Settling down?' This was something Josslyn could just not imagine for herself ... an ordinary, daily domestic routine.

'Bless you! I didn't *have* to stop travelling. Ramón was as footloose as me, thank goodness. For I was a wild, headstrong creature in those days. He could afford to travel. We went everywhere together. Oh, they were good days.' Her blue eyes clouded over. 'Only a few weeks before he died, Ramón told me something I shall never forget. He said, "Thank goodness I had the sense to marry a European woman. There is something in the de Grijalvas ... maybe it is our Spanish blood ... that makes us like our women spunky, independent."'

'And when Juan was born?' Josslyn darted a look at

him, wondering if he would be annoyed by this very personal discussion, whether he agreed with his father's sentiments, but he was immersed in a newspaper.

'He came with us,' Bridget said simply. 'It's only these past few years I've had to slow up. You wouldn't think you'd get arthritis in this climate, would you?'

But Josslyn didn't answer; she'd gone into a dream world, where all the things she craved were possible at one and the same time. Bridget O'Hara, a self-confessed feminist, had found a man, who, though he shared her restless spirit, had also wanted marriage, had admired her independence. Some day, perhaps she, Josslyn, would have the same good fortune.

'I have to go into the City this morning.' It was Juan's voice that brought her out of her reverie, 'So I suggest you relax. But this afternoon I am at your disposal. There are several worthwhile sites within easy driving distance.' He treated her to one of his leg-weakening smiles, but she had no doubt that it was an order.

Josslyn knew better already than to argue with him; but she clenched her hands tightly beneath the table; there was a certain set to her full lips which should have warned him she was not so easily biddable. He was the most infuriating man she'd ever met; also, she conceded, the most fascinating. She was a woman but he treated her like an adolescent incompetent and she had no intention of sitting around twiddling her thumbs, awaiting his permission to move. Besides, if his mother was to be believed concerning the characteristics of the male de Grijalvas, he would only despise her if she showed herself to be a complete doormat. Juan de Grijalva should *not* despise her, she vowed. As soon as his powerful black Cadillac had purred away down the hill towards the city, she told Bridget of her intention, certain that Juan's mother was a kindred spirit and not likely to try and deter her. The Irish blue eyes twinkled sympathetically at her defiance.

'I can see you're a girl after my own heart. But 'tis only fair to warn you, you're playing with fire if you go against Juan's instructions.'

'Did you always obey his father implicitly?' Josslyn challenged.

Again the twinkle.

'No . . . and some rare old rows we had, me and my black Irish temper, him and his cold proud fury. But we always made it up . . .' Her tone faded into regretful reminiscence.

'Yes, well . . . that part if it doesn't come into it, so far as Juan and I are concerned,' Josslyn said, her tone brisk to dispel the image Bridget's words had evoked. 'He has no right to order my movements, so . . . is there a bus or anything that will get me into the city?'

'Sure now, there's no need for that. I've my own little car that I rarely drive these days. 'Twill be grateful for the outing. I'll get you the keys. 'Tis only an idea,' she said hesitantly, 'but perhaps you could be back here before Juan. I'll not be telling him anything, of course.'

Josslyn acknowledged the expediency of this manoeuvre.

'But if by any chance I *am* late, I'll take full responsibility. I'm not scared of your son,' she told Bridget, with a characteristic lift of her chin. But she was scared because, if he willed it, he had the power to rob her of the independence of mind and spirit she valued. Oh yes, she could see danger in the fascination he held for her. She was scared, too, because he showed no inclination to use that potency and she found herself, however unwillingly, needing to succumb to his domination. This realisation made her all the more determined to fight it by any means at her disposal. Thus, not long after Juan's departure, Josslyn, too, left the villa, driving Bridget's small car, a street map of the city on the seat beside her. Remembering her thoughts on arriving in Mexico, she was a little nervous at the idea of mingling with the local drivers, but if she went carefully and steadily ... However, immediately after entering the city proper, she noticed a car park and prudence dictated that she leave the vehicle and continue on foot.

She was glad she had, for, driving, she would never have been able to take in so much of the city's splendours. As it was, she strolled along part of the beautiful tree-lined Paseo de la Reforma, reminiscent of Paris's Champs Elysée. Statues of heroes and statesmen alternated with bronze urns; and, at an intersection, the Reforma widened into a large roundabout, centrally adorned by a monument telling a story of Mexico's shame and her glories. Her map told her that there were four such traffic circles or *glorietas*, but she had no intention, nor the time, to walk the avenue's full eight miles and she retraced her steps, her goal the Museum of Anthropology in Chapultepec Park, where she hoped to absorb Mexico's background and history.

She soon realised she had set herself a mammoth, and impossible, task. It would take days, not hours, to see all that the museum had to offer. The building consisted of a series of chambers, circling a patio, at least half a dozen of its halls devoted to the ancient civilisations of Olmecs, Toltecs, Aztecs and Mayans. But she would come again, she promised herself. No doubt the following days would follow the same pattern, Juan departing on business first thing every morning, giving her a few hours free of his supervision.

She was back at the de Grijalva villa only fifteen minutes before Juan himself, barely time to shower and change. Certainly not enough time in which to rest and shake off the slight dizziness, the fatigue which had suddenly overtaken her on the return journey. It was the altitude, of course, and if Juan ever learned of her unscheduled outing, unscheduled by him, he would be in an unassailable position from which to say, 'I told you so'. At lunch she made a supreme effort to appear calm and relaxed.

'I noticed when I garaged the car that the engine of the Volkswagen was warm,' Juan observed over lunch, his words causing Josslyn to jump guiltily. 'You've been out, *madre mia*?'

'Indeed no,' Bridget assured him, 'But I thought 'twould be no harm for the engine to have a run. It's been standing idle a long time.'

'Mm ... yes. You don't get out much these days. It might be an idea to sell the small car and have Pepe drive you out in the other limousine. I'll see to it.'

'No hurry,' Bridget said hastily. 'I thought Josslyn might like to use it as a runabout ... when you're not available.'

'She'll hardly be here long enough. By the time she's ready for any outings of that nature, I'll be available to accompany her,' he said repressively. 'And in any case the Volkswagen isn't suitable for the terrain she'll be covering. This afternoon,' he turned to Josslyn, 'we go to San Juan de Teotihuacan ... it is only a short distance. But tomorrow, since I am free all day, I suggest we make an early start and visit Palenque.'

'B-but that's hundreds of miles away.'

'I am aware of that!' he said drily, 'which is why it would be impractical to drive. We'll confine such expeditions to remote places where there are no airstrips. At Palenque, however, I can land within a short distance of the ruins.'

'You have your own aeroplane?' Josslyn enquired faintly. This man was full of surprises.

'Naturally!' He seemed surprised at her incredulity. 'Also a helicopter. My work entails considerable travel within Mexico, and flying is by far the most efficient means of transport. I propose that we cover Chichen Itza and Uxmal in the same way.'

It was pleasant to relax and be driven for a change, Josslyn admitted to herself, as they set off on their thirty-mile trip to Teotihuacan, and Juan drove well ...

fast, but she never for a moment felt nervous. She had not fully recovered from the morning's solo exertions and, though she still felt resentment that the next few days had been so arbitrarily planned for her, she hadn't had the energy to protest. She leant back against the pliant leather of the passenger seat and tried to take in what Juan was saying as she fought off an insidious desire to sleep.

'Teotihuacan means "the place where all go to worship the gods". Supposedly it was built by the Toltecs ... but when the Aztecs arrived, the site was totally deserted and considered to be cursed, because no one knew for certain why the original inhabitants had left.'

'Perhaps that was just the story the Aztecs put about?' Josslyn suggested. 'They were a murderous lot, weren't they? Perhaps they just killed off the Toltecs themselves and took over?'

'Murderous? No, not in the way you mean. It's true they offered human sacrifice, but not for the sake of killing. They believed it to be a holy task, necessary to placate the gods they worshipped. If the gods were displeased, there would be no rain or sunshine and therefore no crops. The Aztecs and their cattle would have died of hunger.'

'But that's ridiculous ... superstitious ...'

'*We* know that the seasons and the weather can't be influenced by such practices, but they didn't. They also believed that the gods made men of clay, into which they poured some of their own divine blood. So man had a debt to pay ... human sacrifice nourished the gods, renewed their blood. Is it so different from the Christian belief that God created man from dust, that his son gave his lifeblood to save sinners?'

'But Christians don't make human sacrifice ...' she began, then remembered to whom she was talking, a man whose ancestors had been responsible for the Spanish Inquisition. If her mind had been more alert she might have been capable of further reasoned arguments. As it was, she was glad to remain silent, her eyes closed, until they reached the archaeological site.

'Josslyn? Josslyn!' Juan's hand on her arm startled her and she woke to find him leaning over her. Instinctively she flinched away; in spite of efforts to quench the feeling, she had to admit that his physical proximity still continued to disturb her. 'I'm sorry if I woke you too abruptly,' he said. But she had an uneasy feeling he sensed that there was some other reason for her hasty withdrawal. Then, 'You seem unusually tired.'

'It was the enormous lunch,' she excused herself. 'I'm not used to eating much at midday.'

'Hmm!' Juan sounded disbelieving, but he didn't press the point.

Teotihuacan was certainly impressive and Josslyn wasn't sorry Juan had brought her here. Her camera was in constant use, as she photographed first the huge Pyramid of the Sun, which dominated the site.

'Actually it's several pyramids, one built on the other. The smaller one over there . . .' Juan pointed, 'is the Pyramid of the Moon.'

Between the two ran the Avenue of the Dead, lined with the remains of lesser temples and shrines. Throughout the whole area were repeated strange carvings of a snake-like creature with a feathered crest and necklace of plumes, which also appeared in the huge courtyard, surrounded by other, smaller pyramids, some sculptures so well preserved that they still bore the brilliant paint that had once embellished the whole of the stonework.

'The Plumed Serpent?' Juan said, in answer to her query, 'The creature of the ground and the skies. Yes . . . it's the sign of Quetzalcoatl, the man-god of culture and learning. Present day scholars believe he was really a European who somehow made his way to Mexico, but the Indians believed in him implicitly. They still do. They say that Quetzalcoatl aroused the anger of his fellow gods and had to leave Mexico, in a boat made of snake skins. But before he left he promised to return some day ... and the ancient myths portray him as a white man, blond and blue eyed. That's why, when the Spaniard, Cortes, came, greedy for gold, many Indians saw him as a reincarnation of their god and welcomed him, the biggest mistake they could have made. Later, of course, when Christianity came to Mexico, they believed that Jesus was yet another coming of Quetzalcoatl."

Having photographed the sculptures of the serpent from every angle, Josslyn was eager to make a sketch. Drawings from the original subject had more authority, more immediacy of impact and were always preferable to those done from photos. Besides, there was always the risk of a film being lost or damaged ... and her 'Sketchbook' was to consist of drawings, not photographic plates. She leant against a conveniently placed projection and began work. The sun had warmed the stone, was hot on her face, and it required a real effort of will to concentrate on her work; but at last she was satisfied that she had sufficient details. Glancing sideways at an unusually silent Juan, she saw that his eyes were closed and, for a moment, she took the opportunity of observing him thus relaxed ... something she imagined he rarely did.

He was incredibly attractive and he looked far less autocratic and formidable, the dark lashes, which contrasted strikingly with his blond hair, sweeping down over his tanned cheeks. He looked younger, almost vulnerable; sleep, she supposed, gave everyone that appearance; but it *was* only an outward appearance in his case. She had seen no warmth or softness in Juan de Grijalva, quite the reverse. She found herself wondering if that dark tan extended beneath his clothes, experiencing a very improper desire to know. What on earth was the matter with her? It was men who mentally stripped women, not the other way about. But, despite her self-reproach, she continued to study him.

At last, with a sigh which was half a yawn, she looked away. If *he* could sleep, it wouldn't do any harm for her to close her eyes for a few moments, just to catch up with the rest she was supposed to have been taking that morning . . .

Dry mouth, blurred vision and an impression that her surroundings were vibrating . . .

'Do you realise you've slept for two hours?' She was being shaken awake, not roughly, but certainly briskly. 'I had thought of starting out the day after tomorrow, but obviously it's going to take longer than that to get you acclimatised.'

'No!' She didn't want any more delays. 'I'm perfectly all right. It was the sun,' she excused herself. 'I often fall asleep in the sun at home. And anyway,' she accused, 'you were asleep too.'

'I would remind you that I *have* done a morning's work. In any case I'd merely closed my eyes in thought. I have a great deal on my mind at present.' Of course *he* wouldn't admit to any such weakness as fatigue.

'You *were* asleep,' she scoffed, 'only you're too stubborn to admit it.'

An aggravating little smile played about his mobile mouth.

'And you, of course, are not too stubborn to admit that you were utterly exhausted?' Suspiciously, 'Did you do as I told you this morning, take things quietly?'

She hesitated. Whereas she was quite within her rights, she considered, to do as she pleased, she hated lying.

'So! I see you did not. Well, I shan't enquire into your activities . . . this time. But if you want my help, see that you follow my advice in future.'

To her chagrin, she slept throughout the entire return journey, waking herself only just in time to save Juan the task of doing so, her golden eyes flashing a defiant challenge to him to make any comment. Surprisingly, he refrained, though that irritatingly mocking smile was once more in evidence.

'Did you enjoy Teotihuacan?' Bridget was waiting to greet them. 'You didn't find it too tiring?'

'Not a bit!' Josslyn said firmly, straightening her shoulders, but refusing to look in Juan's direction.

'Good, because we are invited to dine and spend the evening with my mother-in-law. She's heard of you from Juan and myself ... and, no doubt, Manuela ... and she's very anxious to meet you.'

So Juan had spoken of her to his grandmother. What had he said? she wondered. Very little probably; just that they had an Englishwoman staying with them for a few days ... a woman, the responsibility for whose welfare had been inflicted upon him. His grandmother would be of the old school, brought up to respect and defer to men. She would strongly disapprove of the modern woman Josslyn represented, independent, career-minded. How, Josslyn wondered, had Doña Albina reacted to her son Ramón's marriage to Bridie? She would ask Bridget some time, but there was no time now. An invitation from La Abuelita was probably tantamount to a royal command and to be late would be frowned upon. With a sigh, she supposed she had better freshen up and don one of the only two dresses she had brought with her.

It wasn't very difficult to choose between a cream cotton dress and a green one, but nevertheless, Josslyn tried them both on twice, before she decided on the cream. It showed off her lightly tanned skin to better advantage, clung more femininely to her splendid figure. Up until now the de Grijalvas, mother and son, had only seen her in trousers, and once she and Juan started out on their travels, trouser suits would be the order of every day. Not that she was taking care with her appearance for his benefit ... she doubted he'd notice if she wore a sack ... but as a courtesy to his grandmother.

Doña Albina's quarters, though part of the villa, were completely separate, what in England, Josslyn thought, would be called a 'granny flat'. The windows were fitted with a fine mesh screen to keep out insects, a custom her daughter-in-law had not adopted. Bridget liked an unobstructed view from her windows, she said, preferring to use the modern spray repellents on unwelcome intruders.

The door was opened to them by Manuela, black eyes hostile as they rested on Josslyn. She seemed to resent their intrusion, or was it just *her* presence the girl objected to? Josslyn wondered.

Immediately, she had an impression of elegance: woven rugs, wall hangings, heavy furniture. It was like stepping from one culture to another, from Bridget's modernity into the hacienda-like atmosphere of old Spain, and Josslyn braced herself to meet the aristocratic matriarch.

The salon into which Manuela ushered them was a long, high room, with three French windows open on to the terrace. Surprise made Josslyn break step for a moment. Doña Albina was not in the least awe-inspiring. This was no arrogant Spaniard, but a tiny figure dressed in black silk, a little black, fringed shawl of fine cashmere about her narrow shoulders, her skin only a slightly deeper shade of magnolia than Manuela's. There was no doubt that they came of the same race; and this was how the mestizo girl would look in old age.

Señora de Grijalva-Lopez sat in a carved, high-backed chair, at her elbow a small table of inlaid, native woods, on which lay a spectacle case and a diminutive handkerchief edged with fine lace. Despite her obvious great age, her soft skin was still virtually unlined and her hair, once black, now white, was drawn tightly back to display the carved features.

'*Abuela mía*, this is Miss Ransome, the daughter of my friend Joss. You remember Joss?'

The old hand trembled very slightly, as Doña Albina indicated a seat close to herself. The eyes which, apparently, needed spectacles, were shrewd and penetrating, yet curiously enigmatic.

'Sit down, Miss Ransome. Of course I remember Joss, *mi nieto*! A fine man ... a man such as you ... such as your grandfather was.' To Josslyn, 'I was grieved to hear of his sudden death. And so you, Señorita, are his daughter. You are very like him ... tall, good-looking ... in the European way,' The old eyes were suddenly speculative and Doña Albina glanced at her grandson. Josslyn could almost read her thoughts and she could have told the old lady that she need have no fear; her grandson had shown no interest in her. 'Manuela, *chica*,' Doña Albina commanded suddenly, 'tell the servants we will eat.'

'Good!' the girl muttered. 'Already we have put back our meal two hours for La Inglesa and I am hungry.'

'Manuela!' Bridget's tone was sharply reproving, whereas her mother-in-law issued no rebuke. To Josslyn, Bridget explained, 'Normally my mother-in-law eats her evening meal at five ... the old custom. Tonight's delay is not your fault. With our more European ways, Juan and I always dine at seven, as we did last night.'

The sulky Manuela dined with them and Josslyn was continually aware of her brooding, hostile gaze. Here, even in Doña Albina's apartment, she still attempted to monopolise Juan's conversation and the old lady still did not correct her. No wonder Juan looked upon the mestizo girl as a friend, perhaps more? His grandmother evidently regarded her as such, certainly not as a servant. 'In Mexico,' Harry Livings had told Josslyn, 'you either have a servant or you *are* a servant. There are no fine distinctions.' So into what classifications did Manuela really fall?

The fare was simple, including the usual beans and rice. Inevitably tortillas were served, but Josslyn was relieved to find that there was also a conventional soup, a very good steak and a light trifle. The conversation was conducted in English, Doña Albina's accent as impeccable as that of her grandson. For so old a woman, Juan's grandmother had a lively, enquiring mind and she evidenced great interest in Josslyn's work ... how long it was likely to take her, when she would be returning to England? No, Doña Albina was certainly no haughty Castilian lady, though judging by Juan's looks his father's blood and probably therefore his grandfather's must have been more Spanish than Mexican. From his grandmother's side had come the lean, ascetic Indian features, which, combined with the hauteur of the Spaniard, gave him his clean-cut arrogance, the piercing, all-seeing gaze; but the blue of those eyes was Bridie's gift to him.

The evening, after the meal, was a short one. Doña Albina it seemed retired early, but before Josslyn left, the old lady issued one of her commands.

'You will come and see me again, alone, tomorrow ... and we will talk.'

'Not tomorrow, *abuelita mía*!' Juan intervened before Josslyn could answer. 'Tomorrow, I am taking Josslyn to Palenque. The next day, maybe? *Sí*?'

At the mention of their proposed outing, there was a distinctly sibilant hiss from Manuela's direction, but when Josslyn glanced at her the mestizo girl's face was impassive. Only the eyes glittered, alive and strangely reptilian in their unblinking malevolence.

'I wouldn't like her at my back, in the dark, with a knife,' Josslyn thought with an inward shudder.

Though Josslyn would not have admitted it, she was nervous about making a flight in a private aircraft, but from the moment Juan walked purposefully towards the Cessna, clicked switches, turned appropriate dials, she felt a little more confidence in his abilities. She should have known that anything he did he would do well.

Reluctant admiration for him stirred in her.

The engine started and moments later they taxied along the runway. Juan pulled back the stick and suddenly they were airborne, the earth diminishing, the sky receiving them into its cloudless blue. It was, Josslyn found, after all, an exhilarating experience, being in a small plane. No large, impersonal cabin space to come between her and the sky. She felt closer to the elements, more a part of them, and something, some primitive instinct, quivered within her. The flight was made in two stages, with a re-fuelling stop at Tuxtla Gutierrez. From Tuxtla, they flew over vistas of banana, coffee and cocoa plantations, villages . . . and jungle.

'The Mayas are another of Mexico's mysteries,' Juan told Josslyn, as he made an expert three-point landing on the airstrip near the ruins. 'They are quite different from all other Indians. Their present-day descendants are short, with unusually large heads. No one really knows where their ancestors came from, though some historians are anxious to believe the theory that they originated from the lost continent of Atlantis.

'Do you believe that?'

He shrugged muscular shoulders.

'I only believe in what I know for certain. I'm not a romanticist.'

Josslyn could well credit it of a man who wanted no ties, no permanent woman in his life. She saw him as an opportunist, a materialist. Still determined to stress her capabilities, she was out of the light aircraft before Juan could offer assistance and he commented wryly upon her actions.

'I have to admit you're more independent than most of the young women I've met . . . Manuela excepted. But there may come a time when even you will be glad of a helping hand.'

He sounded so complacently assured of this that she resolved there never would be such a moment; and as for Manuela . . . what a half-primitive mestizo girl could achieve, so could Josslyn.

'Maybe when I'm old and decrepit,' she riposted, 'but then *you* won't be around to have the satisfaction of saying you told me so!'

'You? Old and decrepit?' The blue eyes made a comprehensive survey. 'I can't imagine that, somehow. I believe you will grow old very gracefully.' The unexpectedness of a compliment from him made her blush and, to cover her confusion, she said lightly:

'Well I should certainly like to grow old as your grandmother has. She's very beautiful for so old a lady. Her skin's so smooth, so soft looking.'

'Manuela too will be like that in old age,' Juan commented, looking pleased at her praise of Doña Albina. 'Did you know she and my grandmother are distantly related?'

Manuela! Manuela! Always Manuela! Josslyn gritted her teeth. She hadn't known of the relationship between the girl and Doña Albina. It certainly accounted for something which had puzzled her, the old lady's tolerant manner towards her young companion. But she didn't want to talk about Manuela. Something about the mestizo girl, the thought of her, seemed to cast a shadow over the warmth of the sun, for Josslyn experienced a sudden shiver.

The ruins were certainly spectacular, set on their high plateau against the bottle-green background of the mountains soaring above them, the pyramids in sharp contrast to their primordial surroundings.

'If this were the nineteenth century, you would have had to hack your way through the jungle,' Juan commented, 'risked malaria and yellow fever, to see a sight like this.'

Modern transport might have taken the adventure out of Palenque, Josslyn mused, but though she longed for virgin territory, to make her own discoveries, she wasn't sorry Juan had insisted on bringing her here. How her father would have loved Mexico! Surprisingly,

there were significant similarities between this architecture and that he had observed in oriental countries.
In the Temple of the Cross, the sacred tree was almost a
counterpart of that he had sketched in Cambodia, while
sculpted figures and lotus blossoms were almost Hindu-
Buddhist.

Most impressive of all, and Josslyn felt she could
never record sufficient of their beauties in the time
available, were the Temple of the Sun ... a complex
gallery of rooms organised around patios, where
exquisite reliefs portrayed prisoners in submission to
their Spanish conquerors ... and the Temple of the
Inscriptions, containing the funerary crypt of a ruler of
Palenque.

To see this tomb, they had to enter via a triangular
Mayan arch, then descend sixty feet or so down a
narrow, humid stairway in zigzag flights, no longer
guarded, Juan assured her, by the skeletons of the six
'volunteers' who had remained as guardians. Josslyn
shuddered.

'Fancy being buried alive ... and against your will.
They weren't really volunteers, were they? Just to think
of it makes me feel quite ... quite sick.'

The hand placed beneath her elbow was firmly
supporting, his words reassuring, and she could only
hope he attributed her lack of composure to a residue
of distaste, rather than to the shock of awareness his
touch triggered off.

'I'm sure that, like the Egyptian tomb servants, they
would have been drugged, so that they were unaware of
their fate. Come, let's go! The effects of this place must
be very claustrophobic if you're at all nervous ...'

'I'm not in the least nervous.' She refuted the
suggestion, but knew that her protest was unconvincing.
The thought of being immured alive had always
troubled her vivid imagination and she did not shake
off the supporting hand until they emerged once more
into the open air, allowing herself to enjoy ... just for a

few moments, she pleaded with common sense, the
sensual reaction of her body to the pressure of his
fingers.

'A little bare, wasn't it?' Juan commented conversa-
tionally, giving her time to regain her fresh colour. 'The
tomb had to be emptied of its treasures of course, for
security reasons . . . jade masks, necklaces, beads, rings,
pottery . . .'

'Yes, I know! A marvellous collection! They're in the
Musuem of Anthropology in . . .' Josslyn faltered and
bit her lip to prevent herself saying more; but it was too
late.

'You've seen them!' The dark blue eyes narrowed
dangerously and it was a statement, not a question. 'So
that's why you were so tired yesterday! *You* used my
mother's car, *didn't you*?' He snapped out the last two
words.

'Yes!' The toss of Josslyn's silvery head was defiant.
'What of it? I had her permission . . .'

'You also had my advice to remain quietly at the
villa! Are you in the habit of ignoring advice?'

'If I consider it unnecessary . . . uncalled for!'

'And on what vast store of experience did you base
your decision to discount my advice?' His tone was
cutting. 'It doesn't credit you with much common sense,
does it? You know nothing about this country, or its
climate. *I do!* But you chose to ignore what I told you.
You know, I'm beginning to have serious doubts about
the wisdom of this whole thing.'

'This . . .?'

'Your plans to travel into the interior. It's not like
going on a picnic in the English countryside, you know
. . . and if you're so determined to go your own way, no
matter what I say, then as far as I'm concerned, our
arrangement is off . . . cancelled!

CHAPTER THREE

MUCH as it galled her to have to climb down, to apologise, Josslyn knew that, for the sake of her enterprise, she must do so. She was aware of the grudging note in her voice and was sure Juan recognised it; but to her relief, he accepted at face value her assurance that she would be guided by him and attempt to curb her impetuosity, so long as their arrangement might stand.

On their return from Palenque, they were greeted by Bridget with the news that Doña Albina, not to be baulked of her wishes, had sent a message via Manuela that she wished Josslyn to dine with her, alone, immediately she returned.

'Do you mind? Are you too tired?' Bridget had asked anxiously. 'When my mother-in-law sets her mind on something, 'tis hard to divert her.'

'I don't mind,' Josslyn assured her. 'Frankly I find Doña Albina quite fascinating.'

But afterwards, when she thought back over the evening, it was difficult to see any real reason for the Señora's urgency, other than an old woman's whim. Nothing of real importance had passed between them. Their conversation had consisted entirely of questions on the Señora's part and answers on Josslyn's, concerning her private life . . . whether she was engaged, or likely to be . . . and concerning her work, which included suggestions by Doña Albina about areas worth visiting; and for these Josslyn *was* grateful.

'You would find much to interest you in the jungle areas of the east coast. There you could study the Olmecs, my own people . . . a race so ancient that they created the first civilisation of America,' the Señora told

Josslyn proudly. 'They have many ancient rites and traditions. They are great healers . . . magicians.'

Naturally, all this information fired Josslyn with curiosity and enthusiasm, but, where Juan was concerned, she was learning prudence. It would not do to *demand* that he take her into jungle country . . . not yet. She decided to see if their first expedition, to a fiesta in a highland Indian village, planned for the following day, was a success, before she mentioned his grandmother's suggestions. Perhaps she could work Doña Albina into their conversation, ask about his grandmother's origins as if she knew nothing of them, so that the suggestion seemed to come from Juan himself, rather than as a request from Josslyn.

She left Doña Albina's apartment by way of the terrace. It was still early . . . a hot, sultry evening, the air thick, ponderous, dormant, and she felt reluctant to go inside just yet. A stone stairway at the end of the terrace tempted her up on to the *azotea,* the flat roof of the house, with its splendid view down over the sprawling city. The *azotea* had been treated in the same way as the patio, with clusters of containers holding plants and shrubs of every description; it was some moments before Josslyn realised she was not alone . . . and then only because a freak whisper of a breeze brought to her nostrils the pungent scent of a cheroot.

'Is . . . is there . . . who's there?' she asked. The villa seemed secure within its protective walls, but you never knew . . . She was almost relieved when Juan emerged from beyond the screening row of tall, fern-like plants, but she was apprehensive too. Perhaps up here she was trespassing on his private preserves and for the moment she had no wish to displease him again. She would reassert herself a little, she promised her ego which had suffered at having to plead with him, once they were safely on their way. As he strolled towards her, she began a hasty explanation of her presence, but he waved her words aside.

'The *azotea* is for the pleasure of anyone who cares to use it . . . and as you say, it has been a fine evening. But it would be wise to go inside now. The storm is about to break.'

'Storm?' she said disbelievingly. If he wanted to rid himself of her company, surely he could think of some more convincing method. The sky was darkening, but then night did seem to come down rapidly in Mexico. She had seen no signs of bad weather.

Then, even as she began to move away, convinced that he wanted his retreat to himself, in spite of his statement to the contrary, lightning blazed, ran down the sky like the slash of a sword: a violent flare of violet light, which for a few moments illuminated the whole of the city and her surroundings. The garish hue made ghostly, luminous images of the plants and of her companion. Thunder broke, as though great round cannon balls smashed down on the very *azotea* itself, with a force that seemed to make the building shudder, followed by a deluge of rain that brought an icy air with it.

Josslyn gasped with a very real terror. Usually she was unaffected by storms, but that was at home . . . in England. This was very different, surely a storm to end all storms, as though the end of the world were imminent. Without realising that she had done so, she moved towards Juan, involuntarily seeking protection from his masculine strength, a need she would have scornfully refuted under normal circumstances. At once she regretted betraying her fear; she had been so determined not to reveal any weakness to this man who scornfully denigrated women as clinging creatures and she fully expected some scathing remark. But he too seemed to react automatically, his arms closing about her protectively, drawing her towards the shelter of a concrete structure that formed an arbour of sorts.

'It's all right,' he murmured against her hair. 'Be still. It will pass very quickly. No harm will come to you.'

And somehow she found herself believing him, as though she recognised in him a rock of strength to cling to, a rock that even the elements dared not assail. But still she trembled, couldn't stop, for, as the ferocity of the storm began to abate and she was released from the blinding suffocation of her fear, she became aware that other sensations were stealing over her, culminating in a very different kind of panic. Held close to Juan, the scent of him was in her nostrils, a combination of warm, masculine flesh, a hint of aftershave, a lingering trace of the cheroot he had tossed aside as the storm began. He seemed totally calm, matter of fact, a man protecting a frightened, helpless woman. But she . . .? With shocked surprise, she was aware once again of that unexpected sexual tension within herself, which this time was an almost uncontrollable desire to press herself closer to him. Instead, the recognition of the feeling made her draw away, knowing instinctively that she mustn't let *him* feel the body language which would reveal her reaction. Pride forbade it. He had no interest in her; she didn't want his scorn, or his pity. She had claimed as great a disinterest in 'emotional involvements' as his own. But the violence of her physical response filled her with dismay. Despite her resentment of his blatantly authoritative masculinity, she knew that very quality could also, if she were not careful, play havoc with her peace of mind, perhaps her whole future happiness.

She moved away, apologising.

'I'm sorry. I'm not usually so nervous. The suddenness of the thunder and lightning took me by surprise. I . . . I'll see you in the morning then?'

He nodded his acceptance of her explanation, made no attempt to restrain her—why should he?—made no remark beyond,

'I should prefer an early start. We have a long way to go.'

*   *   *

The air of the Mexican highlands was as pure as that of any Swiss Alp as the Land Rover bumped its way along a track that scarred through the fields. The whole valley was a waving sea of plumed maize, broken only occasionally by pepper trees, or a mud-brick village. Up above them, in the bright blue vault of the sky, large birds dipped and wheeled. Josslyn thought it rather a picturesque sight, until she discovered that the birds were vultures, and shudderingly she made comment on this ill-omened sight.

'Not at all,' Juan said. 'There's no need for superstition or for alarm. These birds perform a service. Without them, carcasses would pollute the land and the drinking water, cause outbreaks of disease and epidemic.'

As he was constantly reminding her, there was so much she didn't know about his country. Josslyn admitted it reluctantly, feeling put in her place, a sensation she did not enjoy. She decided that in future she would keep her thoughts and opinions to herself and concentrate on her driving.

For Juan had suggested that she take a turn at the wheel, a test of her capabilities she felt sure, for he was observing her progress critically, as he sat sideways, one arm draped across the back of her seat.

He was wearing khaki coloured trousers and a short-sleeved, bush style shirt, his arms a deep bronze. His free hand rested on the dashboard to steady him against the jolts of their progress. On his forearm, Josslyn had noticed a strange, bluish shape, though she could not make out any precise details. A tattoo, she supposed, though she wouldn't have thought him the type to go in for such immature trivialities.

Though he was not actually touching her, she was tinglingly aware of that arm's encircling presence and she wished he would remove it; it was interfering with her concentration to an alarming extent and she didn't want to give him any cause to criticise her driving, nor did she want him to know how his closeness affected her, making her whole body strangely weak. She found herself unable to forget that incident up on the *azotea* only separated from this moment by a few hours, when she'd received a considerable shock, experienced feelings she hadn't wanted to experience; not a warm, exciting feeling, but, alarmingly, an ache deep down that had troubled her intensely, troubled her because it was an ache that could never be alleviated ... because Juan had not shared the intensity of the moment, had not been aware of her as a woman as she had been of him as a man.

And so, reminded by his present proximity of that brief time spent on the *azotea*, Josslyn tried to divert her thoughts by conversation, however banal it might seem to him. Another rut had almost jerked the steering wheel from her grasp, and dust billowed up around them, drifting in through the open window.

'What an awful road!'

Juan shot her an 'I told you so' glance.

'You'll encounter far worse, believe me. I suggested this particular trip first, because it won't take us too far from Mexico City ... just in case it proves too much for you. You're not fully acclimatised yet, and what you've got in mind for the next three months ... if you last that long ... will be pretty tough going for a woman.'

If she lasted that long! There and then, Josslyn vowed he should never find her lacking in stamina, courage or independence, should never hear the slightest complaint pass her lips. Reluctantly in the first instance, she had agreed to accept his help, since it seemed that with his co-operation doors, figuratively speaking, would be opened to her, where alone she could not expect to enter. But now she had a need to prove herself to him, though she was unwilling to put a name to the motive for that need.

For someone of her determined self-sufficiency, it

had been hard to see all the tasks she had planned for herself taken out of her hands. She'd planned to hire a vehicle, but instead they were using Juan's own Land Rover, the hardiest form of transport for the pot-holed highways, cobblestone streets and the sometimes non-existent roads of· Mexico. The vehicle was fully equipped against all mechanical hazards, even down to aerosol inflators. Garages where tyres could be mended were few and far between.

'Is it much further to the village?' she asked, merely to break the silence that had fallen again. It made her uneasy to have a passenger whose time seemed to be totally spent in assessing her. Was it just her capabilities, of which he still seemed doubtful, her appearance . . . or both?

Without undue vanity, she knew she looked attractive, as well as workmanlike, in sage green denims and matching shirt. But she knew too that she longed for his appreciation of her appearance, as well as his acknowledgment that she was as capable as any man of the task she had undertaken. And if he *should* begin to see her as an attractive woman, the way *she* had suddenly recognised the pull *he* could exert upon her, she thought dizzily, then their expeditions could be fraught with dangers very different to those her mother had foreseen, dangers that gave Josslyn a frisson of pleasurable anticipation.

'Not much further,' he answered her question. 'Just beyond the next settlement. Why? Tired already? Want me to drive again?'

'Certainly not!' she retorted indignantly. 'I'm just anxious to get there and get on with my work, since you've already held me up for two or three days.' It was just as well he was capable of annoying her too. If he once suspected her true feelings towards him, he would be on his guard against her. Oh, if he could only be brought to admire her for her self-sufficiency, perhaps there was just a chance . . .

Ahead of them now, the land humped up into foothills, beyond them the apex of a volcano showed, its upper crater still tipped with snow. The dirt track . . . by no means could it now be dignified by the name of road . . . ran through a village, where houses hemmed their vehicle in so closely that it was sometimes necessary for Josslyn to reverse in order to negotiate a corner. In the middle of a desolate, dirt square, a man, wrapped to the eyes in a blanket and wearing a wide-brimmed hat, leant motionlessly against the trunk of a solitary pepper tree. Involuntarily, Josslyn laughed.

'Mañana! A typical Mexican scene.'

'By no means,' Juan retorted. 'You only think so, because the artist and the photographer have constantly portrayed him this way. You, I hope, will have more insight, more imagination by the end of your stay. This man was probably up well before dawn. Contrary to popular belief, the average Mexican is not an idle layabout; he's hard working, grinding away like merry hell from dawn to dusk. He has to, just to survive!'

His tone was that of a reprimand, calculated, she felt sure, to make her feel both guilty of discourtesy to one of his countrymen and ignorant of custom at the same time. But if he thought she was going to apologise for what had, after all, only been a light-hearted remark . . . Outwardly he might be absolutely stunning, disruptively attractive, but what about his inner personality? Had he no humour? She drove on in grim silence. It would be dreadful to discover that, in spite of all his attractions, he was totally unlikeable, totally inhuman.

The track was becoming almost non-existent now and she had to drive carefully as they overtook peasants, some on foot, some on horseback, all heading in the same direction as themselves. The land was sharply undulating, cornfields, broken by tracts of wasteland, through which a straggling river made its way. Then, abruptly, even the track ended, blocked by massive boulders.

'This is where we have to leave the Land Rover,' Juan announced.

'You mean walk ... with all this gear?' As soon as the words were out, she regretted them. His amused glance accused her of faint-heartedness and, to dispel this ideal, she scrambled at once from the vehicle and made no comment about the weight of her share of the burden. She had expected to have to buy, or hire her own tent, but again, airily, Juan had informed her that he was sufficiently well equipped to mount their expeditions.

They climbed on for several miles through the hills, Juan exchanging pleasantries, which Josslyn could not understand, with the peasants they overtook. For he set a fast pace, deliberately testing her again, she suspected. About two hours later, they reached an upper valley; and now the volcano rose directly above them ... extinct, Juan assured her, as if he thought she might be apprehensive. Golden marigolds and banks of blue lupins edged the track and ahead of them the sunlight glinted on the flat roofs of houses and outlined the roof of a tiny, whitewashed church. Civilisation, Josslyn thought, somewhat ashamed of her heart's leap of relief at the blissful anticipation of rest and refreshment.

But it was premature. Close to, what had looked an impressively large settlement was merely a collection of mud cottages, their baked bricks crumbling.

'How on earth do these people manage to exist?' she asked, for the standard could scarcely be very high in this remote, barren-looking area.

'With great difficulty! They're farmers of a sort.' Juan gestured towards an enclosure made of long, slim logs. 'At night they corral their animals, to fertilise an area of soil where they will plant crops. Tomorrow that enclosure will be moved to another section of land. Their cows pull the plough, the goats give them their milk and cheese, the sheep wool.'

'And meat as well, of course.'

'No.' He looked at her doubtfully, as if assessing her for squeamishness. 'They trap field mice ... and they hunt deer ... and squirrels.'

Josslyn could not prevent her nose from wrinkling slightly; but if he was expecting any stronger reaction, he was going to be disappointed. She hoped devoutly, however, that if they were offered any food it would not fall into the mouse or squirrel category or, if it did, that Juan would not enlighten her.

'And now,' Juan pointed directly ahead of them, 'the fiesta we have come to see.'

He had told her they were going to a fiesta, but Josslyn's expectations she realised now had been out of all proportion to reality. This was not a large, important event, which drew tourists from all over the country. It seemed to be very much a local affair.

Young men and girls paraded in their best finery, children ran everywhere, while babies were carried in the long, woven silk *rebozos* of their mothers. Horsemen cavorted, their ponies' hooves raising the ever-present dust. A few old women sold tacos from primitive stalls; and the chief entertainment seemed to be provided by the guitars some of the men carried, the jangling of the church bells and the occasional eruption of a firecracker.

But then she reproached herself for her feeling of disappointment. If she'd been looking for sophistication, there was plenty to be found in the cities. *This* was what her trip was all about ... the recording of little known customs of the simple, the ordinary folk. But again her longing to begin work was forestalled.

'Don't set out your sketching materials yet. On arrival it's considered courteous to call on the chief citizen and take some refreshment with him. And remember, exercise tact. The indigenes don't think of themselves as Mexicanos in a national sense. They call themselves by their old tribal names and speak their own language ... sometimes even to the exclusion of

Spanish. They don't "cotton much" to strangers, as our North American neighbours put it.'

Though impatient of yet more delay, Josslyn was not unwilling to pause for refreshment. Loath to admit it, she was still finding the high altitude fatiguing and the long uphill climb on foot had increased her discomfort.

By some means, the chief citizen of this remote village had received advance warning of their arrival. Now he approached solemnly and he and Juan brushed palms in greeting.

'*Eliseo, amigo! Como está usted?*' Juan greeted their host man to man, but Josslyn noticed with some perplexity the other man's obvious deference. He treated Juan with what amounted almost to ... reverence? It seemed though that he knew something of the outside world, for he spoke halting Spanish, wore Levis and a store bought shirt. Josslyn was frank in her disappointment.

'I didn't think civilisation would have extended this far. I was hoping to get photographs and sketches of typically native costumes.

Juan nodded. 'I too deplore the disappearance of tradition. The Indians need help, but of a practical kind: improved farming techniques, health care. But they don't need civilisation as we know it. In fact, whole tribes have already been wiped out by the white man's corruption and disease.' Then he smiled. 'But don't worry. The veneer of civilisation is still very thin. I'm sure Eliseo will be delighted to pose for you in any guise you wish. What man could refuse so charming an artist?' The smile which so transfigured his lean, ascetic face was accompanied this time by a sweepingly comprehensive study of her, from top to toe.

Josslyn found herself colouring up. Was he being sarcastic, or was his compliment genuine? Somewhat cynically, Harry Livings had commented that the only time a Mexican went out of his way to praise or flatter a woman was when he was planning a campaign of seduction; but that could hardly be so in Juan's case. She decided to pass off his remark with a shrug and a politely incredulous smile.

The home of the chief citizen had little to recommend it over the others, except for a few drooping dahlias in the dry soil surrounding it. Bedroom, parlour and kitchen all shared space in the one large, chimneyless room. The dining corner was plastered with red earth, to distinguish it; and in the area set aside as a kitchen, the wall was ornamented with pottery, kettles and wicker baskets. Below these was a beehive-shaped, adobe oven, which would soon be baking the tortillas and unleavened maize cakes presently being prepared by Eliseo's wife and daughters.

In this inadequate accommodation lived the chief, his wife, two grown girls, four boys and a baby in arms. However did they exist? Josslyn wondered with a mingling of horror and compassion. One of the girls brought chairs, whilst her father fetched glasses and a bottle of tequila, obviously kept only for honoured guests, because Eliseo himself drank *pulque* ... the poor Mexican's beer.

This was the second day of the fiesta ... Juan translated Eliseo's explanation. Yesterday there had been cock fighting. It had been good sport. Much blood had been spilled. Today there would be steer riding. Eliseo was asking Juan if he would take part.

'A-and ... w-will you?' Josslyn felt a stab of fear. On television, she had seen steers ridden in American rodeos and it looked a very dangerous affair. Today there might not be blood alone, but broken bones too ... Juan's bones.

'Of course.' Juan sounded unconcerned. 'It would be considered very bad manners to refuse such an invitation.'

Josslyn fought against the urge to protest further. Juan wouldn't thank her for indulging in concern for his safety; but the knowledge of what he intended to do continued with her as an uneasy sensation in the pit of her stomach. Pull yourself together, she adjured herself sharply. He feels nothing for you. He's your guide, an unwilling as well as an unwanted one at that. All right, you don't want to see the man hurt, but he's given you no excuse to feel such personal concern ... and it's not as if you couldn't find your way back to the city alone. If he were to incapacitate himself ... only slightly of course ... it would get him out of your hair. But suppose his injuries weren't slight? Suppose ... suppose he broke his neck? For some reason that *would* matter to her ... a lot. Why? These thoughts went endlessly round in her mind, as, proudly, Eliseo gave them a conducted tour of his village, around the crumbling huts, with their open doors marking dark interiors, into which it was impossible to see. The sturdiest building was that of the schoolhouse, a new looking, pre-fabricated building, with adjacent quarters for a resident teacher.

For the first time, Eliseo addressed Josslyn directly, pointing first to the building and then to Juan.

'*Escuela! Regalo! El Señor! Bueno, bueno, la serpiente pluma ... Quetzalcoatl.*'

Doubtfully, Josslyn looked at Juan. The final word was familiar to her, the name of Juan's antique shop, but ...

'I think I understand some of it? He's saying the school is a gift ... from you? But the rest of it? What did it mean?'

'Yes! I was responsible for the school ... a nothing ... a poor thing. As to the rest ... a mere fantasia ... a nonsense not worth translating!' His manner was brusque, as if he wished Eliseo had not imparted his information; and with what was an obvious change of subject, he asked Josslyn if she would like to see inside the church. She followed obediently, but he could not distract her thoughts so easily. Was Juan de Grijalva something of a philanthropist then, using the vast profits he probably made from his antiques? And did his interest lie in just this one village, or was it more universal?

Inside, the church was dark, cold, musty, with a smell that resembled incense but was not. As her eyes accustomed themselves to the dimness, she could make out the lines of the altar, decorated with white flowers ... but flowers that were past their best. There was no service in progress, yet figures were moving in some strange, ritualistic dance, their feet drumming on the beaten earth floor. They were watched by motionless, white clad girls. The dancers, she saw, now that her eyes were accustomed to the light, were men, their clothes dark, their faces crudely masked. One man held a stick, carved with a snake's head, its jaws realistically articulated.

'Damn!' Josslyn heard Juan's expletive and he took her arm, trying to draw her back outside. 'You don't want to see this.'

But she did. She resisted him. Who was he to monitor what she did or did not watch? Yet afterwards, she wished she had taken his advice.

Mingled with the incense-like smell and the heavy perfume of decaying flowers, there was the stale odour of sweat, the sourness of beer. As the men danced, they plucked at the girls' dresses and the man with the snake made threatening passes at their faces. At the sight of Juan a little murmur ran through the group of dancers ... *'la serpiente pluma'* ... and they moved towards the couple in the doorway, their gestures seeming to defer to Juan.

Something about the ritual made Josslyn uneasy and as the dancers drew near to her, peering into her face muttering the word 'Itzpapalotl', she moved back with a little gasp. Men and children laughed, but to her, despite the ecclesiastical setting, the whole thing reeked of evil, filled her with primitive superstition. She was only too ready now to respond to the urging of Juan's hand on her arm.

'What does it mean?' she asked Juan as they left the building. 'Surely that has nothing to do with religion?'

'Of a kind,' he said shortly. 'It was a fertility rite. Here they have retained only some aspects of Christianity. They perform the old rituals too.'

'But the priest? Doesn't he mind them using the church like that?'

'There isn't a priest. A place this size doesn't warrant a permanent one any more. The villagers may hear mass once a year ... if they're lucky.'

And meantime they reverted to pagan practices, she thought with a shudder. Surely Juan, product of a Spanish hidalgo and a good, Irish Catholic mother could not approve? And yet he seemed at ease with the people, friendly.

Back at Eliseo's home they were invited inside to eat with the family. The only furnishings consisted of roughly made chairs, a table and a large bed. Apparently the rest of the family slept on *petates* ... mats. In a dark corner was a home altar, decorated with an array of religious figures ... Christian and pagan mingled. Only the men sat at table. Women, Josslyn found with indignation, waited first upon their menfolk, then either stood or sat upon the hard earthen floor to eat their own food. Eliseo's women seemed to take it for granted that Josslyn would wait on Juan and, while she seethed inwardly, she could only comply, remembering his strictures on adhering to local custom.

The fare was good, she had to admit, if somewhat spicy for her palate. There was no mention of mouse or squirrel; instead there was chicken, hot tortillas and beans, served with rice and chillies. The family ate to the accompaniment of noisy conversation in which Juan joined, and the afternoon was half over by the time they finished eating. But, at last, outside, the rumble of hooves and wild shouting announced the arrival of the steers for the fiesta and Josslyn felt a renewal of her anxiety. Would Juan really go through with it?

By the specially prepared stockade, a large crowd had gathered, the men draped in *serapes* ornamented with gay, indigenous patterns, the women with their soft, sequined *rebozos* drawn closely about head and shoulders, against the rapidly cooling mountain air.

The competitors were mostly young men . . . younger than Juan. Mounted on ponies, they were showing off, chasing the steers, leaning out of their saddles to catch at flying tails. The contest began and Josslyn, camera at the ready, watched as the men tried unsuccessfully to remain for the allotted time on the bouncing steers, whose aim was to shake off and gore their tormentors. Juan moved towards the rails.

'You don't really mean to try it? It's dangerous!' Her tone was unconsciously pleading, as unthinkingly, eyes unknowingly eloquent, she laid a hand on Juan's bare arm.

His mouth twisted in a wry smile and for an instant a strong, brown hand covered hers in warm reassurance, sending a *frisson* of sensation along her nerves.

'Women. They are all the same! Don't worry about me!'

'I'm not worried!' she denied sharply, untruthfully, afraid that she'd given herself away. 'If you want to break your neck, that's your business.' Hurriedly, she withdrew her hand, surreptitiously rubbing the back of it across her denims, as though she could banish the pleasant feeling his touch had provoked. But despite her denial, she still watched anxiously, as a steer with a rope around its neck was dragged up against the inside of the stockade and Juan jumped from the top rail on to its back, grasping the rope with both muscular hands.

As soon as the men who were restraining the animal let go, it bucked off into the arena, hitting the ground with all four hooves simultaneously as it tried to rid itself of its unwanted burden. With every jarring leap, Juan was bounced a foot into the air and Josslyn winced as each time he thumped down on the knobbly bony ridge of the creature's back. Flicking its hind legs in the air, the beast then attempted to dislodge him by shaking its body in a violent twist.

The crowd watched these antics with an intense, hushed concentration . . . there was no cheering or cries of encouragement. Then, though it had seemed an impossible task, Juan tamed his mount to a standstill and his trial was over. Josslyn had been so nervously engrossed that she hadn't taken a single photo and she was sure that her face must be pale with her anxiety. But she had time to recover herself as now the men and women crowded around the hero of the hour, repeating over and over again that strange phrase, *'la serpiente pluma, bueno, bueno'*.

When the last of the competitors had been thrown from his steer, the fiesta and indeed the day itself was over, the sun sinking behind the mountains, the volcano only a menacing black outline against the sky.

'Tired?' Juan asked Josslyn.

'A little,' she admitted cautiously. To deny her fatigue altogether would be to arouse his scepticism.

'But not too tired to see another spectacle, of a different kind, before we set up our camp?' Was it a challenge she detected in his tone of voice, or was it genuine concern for her welfare?

'No, not too tired.' But she sighed inwardly and set her teeth as he went ahead, leading the way up a path, winding steeply through a pine forest. She was more tired than she had thought, mostly the altitude, but perhaps also reaction to the tension she had just experienced. She tried to stifle the gasping breaths that forced themselves up from her straining lungs; and at last they reached the summit and stood on the edge of a great natural terrace. Below them, in the distance, the valleys stretching away to the blue ribbed, flat flanked mountains above Mexico City, were bathed in the last blood red of the sunset.

'Well?' Juan demanded.

'Very spectacular.'

'Worth all your effort?' There was sly laughter in his tone and somehow she found herself smiling back at him, suddenly not minding that he had guessed how much the climb had taken out of her.

'Yes . . . well worth it.'

In a sudden gesture of camaraderie, for that was all it was, she assured her leaping heart . . . he would have done the same to any male companion who had shared his climb, this exhilarating experience . . . he flung an arm about her shoulders. But it was more difficult to act as if the demonstration meant no more to her than if they *had* been both of the same sex. She was too aware for comfort of the weight of his arm, of its very masculine warmth, his thigh just brushing hers. Did he feel nothing, absolutely nothing? As for herself, the motive whose existence she had so far endeavoured to ignore was becoming uncomfortably clear. She was in danger from far more than just a physical attraction. Common sense now told her to break the contact . . . before he sensed the tremulousness she fought to control. Oh damn it! Damn the man! She didn't want this complication, especially since he had made all too clear his own policy of non-involvement. It would be humiliating if he should suspect just how much she was attracted to him. Casually, with a yawn that was not altogether feigned, she moved away. It had been a long, full day.

When they reached the village once more, a poplin drill tent had already been erected between two of the mud-brick dwellings, the work of their hosts, Josslyn thought gratefully. But *one* tent? She came to a sudden halt.

'Where's the other tent?' A frightening suspicion seized her, a suspicion that, while it caused apprehension, also tightened the muscles of her stomach in a spasm that was almost excitement.

'There is no other tent. We share.'

'We most certainly do not!' For the sake of

appearances she must protest though the breath caught in her throat at the obvious futility of her objection.

'*Por Díos!*' Juan swore. 'Don't start behaving like an affronted virgin, not at your age. It's a tent we're sharing, not a bed. The sleeping bags are separate.'

What did he mean, at her age? Did he think, just because she was twenty-five, that she was no longer a virgin?

'I thought you said you had enough equipment for two!' Josslyn accused him. 'I was quite prepared to hire a tent for myself.'

'One tent is sufficient, especially when it has to be carried. We won't always be able to get the Land Rover as close to our destination as we have today. And though you won't admit it, of course, you found the walk up here quite arduous enough, without an addition to your load.'

'I . . . I can't share a tent with you,' she reiterated. 'I'm entitled to privacy. I'll . . . I'll find somewhere else.' But it was not the lack of privacy to which she objected; rather it was the dangers of proximity.

'Very well! Perhaps you'd like to accept Eliseo's invitation?' he said mockingly.

Courteously, the chief had offered them the hospitality of his own home, though how he would have fitted them in among his numerous family, Josslyn could not imagine.

'Why don't you accept and I'll use the tent?' she returned smartly.

'Because Eliseo's invitation was only made out of politeness. I wouldn't dream of inconveniencing him.'

'But you don't mind inconveniencing me! You're no gentleman, that's for sure!'

'A "gentleman"?' he laughed, 'to your "lady"? I had the impression that you were something of a feminist. Obviously it doesn't go very deep. If you really believed in sex equality, you wouldn't have any qualms about sharing a tent with me, any more than with another

woman. Besides, I thought I'd already made it pretty
clear I've no designs on your virtue . . . far from it.'

Oh how he twisted things to his own ends. There was
just no arguing with him and did he have to be so
unflatteringly outspoken about her lack of attraction
for him . . . when *she* was so vulnerable?

'But if you find the situation so intolerable, we'll
break camp and head back for Mexico City . . . call the
whole thing off.'

So that's what he was up to. He was trying to wriggle
out of the arrangement he had insisted on. If she had
never met Juan she could very well have managed this
trip alone, would never have had her peace of mind so
endangered. Now he was trying to make her give up her
plans, so that he could accuse her of inadequacy. No
way was he going to succeed.

Without another word, Josslyn marched towards the
tent, her only regret that it was impossible to maintain
her taut, upright posture, that she had to go on hands
and knees to enter.

The two air mattresses had been inflated and set out
side by side, the sleeping bags spread on top.
Ostentatiously, she edged the matresses apart. She was
just wondering how she would manage about undres-
sing, when, to her profound relief, Juan announced
brusquely that he would share a last cheroot with
Eliseo. She was surprised by this concession, but not
knowing how long he would allow her, her bedtime was
a rather scrambled affair, so that in the end she had
plenty of time to lie there, tension coiling tighter within
her, as she waited for Juan to reappear. If he made so
much as one suggestive remark, she'd . . . she'd . . .

When he did enter the tent, she rolled over, her face
to the side, trying not to imagine what every little sound
portended as he undressed. At least he didn't seem to be
in a talkative mood and finally he extinguished the
lantern and she knew he was safely in his sleeping bag.
Now she could relax, except that she was sharply

conscious of his presence, the even tenor of his breathing only a few inches away, aware that this was the first time she had ever shared any accommodation, let alone anything so cramped, with a man. Either one of them had only to stretch out a hand to touch the other; a restless night could even bring them into contact ...! She had been tired, but now it was impossible to sleep. It was too quiet. She felt she had to say something and the subject that most exercised her mind at present was her invidious position ... invidious surely in the sight of others? She knew that on her side this arrangement had been forced on her by circumstances, was perfectly innocent, purely practical so far as Juan was concerned, but ... She cleared her throat.

'What about Eliseo and his wife?' she asked. 'Won't they ... won't they think it strange that we don't have two tents?'

'Why should they find it strange?' He didn't sound drowsy either. 'They assume you are my woman.' The outrageous words made her quiver with shock.

'What? Oh! Oh no! But ...' He couldn't mean it.

'In Mexico, once a man has slept with a woman, she is considered to be his personal property. It would be considered in bad taste to comment or to interfere. They assume that, as we sleep together, we have done so before.'

'You mean ... they think that ... that we ... But why couldn't you simply tell them the facts?' she finished indignantly.

'That I share a tent with you but that you remain untouched?' His tone was ironic. 'They would see that as a poor compliment to your femininity ... or as a decided doubt of my virility.'

'To hell with *your* image,' she retorted hotly. 'Oh, I daresay you just love being given the VIP treatment, but what about *my* reputation? I suppose it never occurred to you that I might object to being taken for your woman?'

'Taken?' he queried. 'Do you mean "taken" in the literal sense?'

'You know very well I don't!' she snapped. 'Your English is perfect. You understand exactly what I mean . . .'

'Yes . . . yes, of course I understand. Relax, Josslyn.' His voice became low pitched; but if it was meant to be reassuring, she didn't feel at all reassured; his husky tones caused something inside her to curl insidiously, longingly. 'Why do you have this feeling of insecurity?' he asked. 'Don't you trust me?' His voice, not as cool and clipped as usual, but faintly husky.

It was herself she was beginning to distrust, Josslyn mused . . . and it wasn't at all flattering to think that he wasn't even disturbed by her presence; but, she reminded herself sternly, she should be glad that it was so. If he were to feel as she did now, there would be only one conclusion. But there was something she wanted . . . needed to know.

'Have you . . . have you ever brought anyone else here?' She found herself holding her breath, waiting for his answer.

'You mean . . . women?' He sounded faintly amused.

'Well . . . yes, I suppose so.'

'Yes I have!' His reply was uncompromisingly matter-of-fact and she had no doubt of its truth. Why should she have? But still there was that dragging feeling of disappointment . . . of jealousy? Stupid to imagine there had never been any women in Juan's life. He might not want to commit himself to any one woman, but he must have experienced a man's natural needs . . . and being the arrogant man he was, he would have fulfilled them. What had Bridget said? So many women had scorched themselves at his flame.

'Why?' Was that mockery in his voice? 'Did you believe, perhaps hope, that you were the first?'

'I couldn't care less how many women you've brought here,' she denied swiftly. 'It just seems a bit hypocritical, that's all ... the way you went on about women not being physically up to this sort of thing.'

'The women I brought here,' he said softly, 'were my mother ... and Manuela. Does that make you feel any better?' His voice sounded nearer; and she peered into the darkness; had he shifted his position? She was almost certain he had. The tent was small enough, but now it seemed smaller. She couldn't seem to breathe. Could she be developing claustrophobia? she wondered wildly. Was it something that came on you suddenly like this?

She was appalled to find herself wanting to find him closer, wanting to turn on to her side, to completely bridge the gap she herself had created.

'Why should *that* make any difference?' She tried to sound uncaring. She didn't mind about Bridget. She was Juan's mother and a seasoned traveller. But she found she did mind about Manuela.

'Because they are both accustomed to this kind of life ... my mother because of her travels with my father, Manuela because she was born to it.'

'And did they have to share your tent?' she enquired sarcastically.

'Naturally. If it's any consolation, Josslyn, you're the first complete novice I've allowed to travel with me.'

Consolation! He'd allowed her to accompany him! It was the other way about, except that she'd had no choice in the matter. He'd forced his company on her. She couldn't resist reminding him of the fact.

'And I didn't need company.'

'No? From what I hear from Harry Livings, you've led a pretty sheltered life up till now, never exposed to any risks. Life is full of risks, you know ... *real* life ... and unsuspected dangers.'

'I was quite prepared to fend for myself!' she retorted hotly. 'Whatever you may think, I'm not a helpless ninny. What danger could I possibly be in?'

'Fending ... perhaps ... what about *defending*

yourself in a country where most men believe a woman
has only one function? Do you think . . . if you'd been
alone . . . if they hadn't believed you to be my property
. . . that Eliseo's young men would have been so
restrained in their behaviour towards you? Now, just
suppose that *I* were to take it into my head to see if
there's anything more to you?'

'Any . . . anything m-more?' Her mouth went dry.
Intuition told her what he meant.

'Mmm. Whether there's anything of the feminine
about you . . . as well as the feminist. Whether that
lovely face and body can be aroused by another kind of
passion than the sort you give to your work. How
would you defend yourself then?'

So he found her face and body attractive. He *had*
noticed her as a woman. She took a deep breath.

'The way I'd defend myself against any unwanted
attentions from a man. B-but I . . . I wouldn't have
to . . .' Suddenly she felt far from confident. 'Because
you . . . you wouldn't . . .'

'But perhaps I would!' Was he just teasing her, or did
he mean it?

'Y-you told me,' she said desperately, 'that you don't
go in for . . . for emotional involvements.'

'True! Not permanent ones. But I'm no more averse
to casual encounters than the next man. I'm quite
normal . . . in case you had any ideas to the contrary. I
may be opposed to the marriage trap, but I've no
objection whatsoever to sexual gratification. In fact I'm
all for it. I assume you have the normal inclinations of a
woman? That you've had men friends?' He sounded as
if the answer was of considerable interest to him.

'Plenty!' she croaked. She didn't want him to think
she was desperate for male attention, that . . .

'So when did you last sleep with a man?'

Josslyn felt as if she'd been punched below the belt.

'Come, you need not be shy. You are not
inexperienced. You too have managed to escape all

permanent entanglements. It would seem we are of the same mind ... two of a kind. You are a practical young woman, so you keep telling me ... no romantic, any more than I am.'

'No, I ...' Her voice didn't seem able to follow her bidding and he took her stammered words for agreement.

He *had* moved closer and he must have the eyesight of a night-time predator for, even in the total darkness, unerringly, his hand had found the curve of her cheek, slid down her neck to her shoulders, awakening a torrent of feeling, making her yearn for its further invasion. Suddenly the sleeping bag seemed no protection at all. In fact it was a snare that hampered her escape. Only she didn't think she wanted to escape ... now. She wasn't sure of anything any more. Her heart was thumping against her ribcage so hard that surely Juan too must be aware of its irregular activity.

'So I'm sure neither of us would want to miss such a heaven sent opportunity.'

What had heaven to do with it? she thought a trifle hysterically. Surely it was Satan who was the tempter? The warmth of Juan's breath was the briefest of warnings, before his mouth found hers. His kiss was just as she had always known it would be, from the first moment she'd felt his attraction ... compelling, exciting ... seductive. But this was dangerous, as their conversation had been dangerous ... provocative in its content ... and it seemed it was up to her to put an end to the situation, before things got out of control. She couldn't really blame Juan for his mistaken assumption; she hadn't exactly attempted to contradict him, not wishing to appear naïve and ingenuous. But this pride could prove to be her very downfall. This body chemistry ... she *could* resist it, if she willed it so. It was only chemistry, wasn't it? It couldn't possibly go any further ... any deeper? The very idea threw her into such a state of alarm that she tried to roll away, but the sleeping bag ... and a strong arm ... hampered her.

'Don't turn coy on me now,' he murmured. 'Tell me you want me, as I want you. I know you do . . . it's been obvious, right from the start . . . but I'd still like to hear you say it.'

It was humiliating to discover that, all along, he had known of her body's leaping response to him. How had she betrayed herself? She thought she had been so careful.

'Why?' she cried disbelievingly. 'Why should you want *me*? A few hours ago you didn't particularly like me. I was just a nuisance . . .'

'Didn't I?' His lips and teeth tantalised the lobe of her ear, explored the curve of her jaw, making her body jerk spasmodically. 'Are you sure of that?'

'Yes,' she managed the whisper. 'You were exasperated at having to act as bear leader to an inexperienced woman . . .' In the darkness she flushed. 'I mean . . . inexperienced as a traveller. If you could have sent me packing, back to England, you'd have done it.'

'But you insisted on staying . . . and you haven't denied that you want me . . . that you were jealous when you thought I'd brought other women here.'

'Well I'm denying it now,' she retorted . . . and she had to, or face the consequences, which could only end in hurt for her. 'You flatter yourself, Juan de Grijalva. Jealousy implies a far deeper interest than a need for mere sexual gratification as you call it. It implies a desire for something far more permanent . . . and I couldn't care less who you've brought here.'

In the darkness she felt his shrug.

'That's fine by me . . . so we can settle for the sex . . . and no strings.' The zip of her sleeping bag offered no resistance to his practised fingers, but it freed her hands for greater resistance, when all she wanted to do was to use them to caress . . .

'You're . . . you're despicable,' she forced herself to say. 'Before we came out here, you were full of talk about how safe I was from your attentions . . . almost insultingly so.'

'Ah . . . so you minded that?' Lightly his fingers rested on her pulsing throat.

'No, no I didn't,' she gasped, fighting for sanity. 'I was . . . relieved. You don't attract me . . . so will you kindly confine our relationship to business . . . as *you* stipulated.'

'Certainly . . . if you're *sure* that's what you want.' But he hadn't released her and his thumb was still stroking the hollows at the base of her throat.

'Of . . . of course I'm sure.' Even she knew her voice did not carry conviction.

'Yet a few hours ago,' he said musingly, 'you seemed touchingly concerned for my safety . . . anxious to prevent me from risking my neck. I could have sworn I felt the bonds of possessiveness tightening around me.'

'Don't be so ridiculous! Oh, but you're horribly conceited!' Summoning all her resolution, she pushed his hands away. 'Fancy being so big-headed that you imagine every woman you meet wants to marry you. Frankly, if you must know, my concern was purely selfish,' she lied. 'If anything had happened to you, I wasn't sure I could find my way back to civilisation.'

'I see!' Was it her imagination, or did he sound almost angry? 'So now we know where we stand . . . and you'll be glad to know that you've successfully passed the test.'

What on earth did he mean by *that*?

He rolled away from her, putting the width of the tent between them once more, his voice languidly cynical.

'I had to be sure, didn't I, that you had no illusions about me . . . about this trip? My mother I know would welcome a European daughter-in-law. Who knows what ideas she might have put into your head. And from what Harry Livings told me . . .' He broke off tantalisingly, but she wasn't going to be drawn into demanding his meaning. He meant to tell her anyway. 'He said you had a father fixation,' Juan continued. 'That you'd never settle for a man who wasn't cast in *his* mould ... an adventurer ... a wanderer. I was rather afraid you might have decided I qualified. He also told me about your mother. She sounds a typical clinging vine, making a drama of Joss's every departure ... and incidentally of yours. No doubt you take after her?'

Josslyn knew Harry would never speak of her or of her mother in that way. He might have told Juan some of the facts, but Juan was deliberately twisting his words, to hurt, to provoke. If only he had not managed to get beneath her guard. But at least there was no need for him to know it.

'My mother,' she said coldly, 'is a very brave woman. Yes, she did hate my father being away, but she never once tried to stop him going ... and yes, I *did* love my father, very much, but not in the unnatural way you're implying. If I *were* looking for a man like him ... and I don't admit that I am ... you wouldn't come anywhere near the standard. He was a great man, a good man, a wonderful husband and father. I doubt if you have it in you to be either. I despise your values. In fact, if it wasn't for my responsibilities to Harry, I'd go back to the city, with or without your help, and take the first plane home. As it is, from now on, I should prefer it if we confined our conversation to Mexican history and custom.'

'And good night to you too!' he said mockingly.

CHAPTER FOUR

THE intense heat struck down, penetrating the straw hat protecting Josslyn's head, and she felt herself break out in a prickly sweat. The deep undergrowth, though it formed walls on either side of the narrow track, gave no protection from the sun, now directly overhead. The dense vegetation gave off a monotonous steam bath, the air so thick with heat it was almost tangible; but Josslyn dared not remove any layers of protective clothing, in case of bugs or poisonous bushes. The colours around her would scarcely be believed, she thought, when she used them on her palette . . . the light sapphire of the sky, the varying shades of viridian and monastral greens.

Juan kept up his usual fast pace and she was too stubborn, too full of pride, to call a halt, or to ask him to slow his effortless stride. She dared not lag behind, for the track divided constantly, changing direction every few moments. If she allowed him out of her sight, she would almost certainly get lost.

'The jungle changes people,' Juan had warned her. 'You will know what it's like to be driven to the limits of your endurance.'

She knew what he meant now. Not normally of a nervous disposition, she found sudden sights and sounds in the undergrowth constantly startling her; monkeys and wild birds seemed to abound and the air was full of their noise. The prickly, damp heat making her irritable. She found herself regretting the slightly cooler air of Eliseo's highland village. Though they had spent only the two days there, she had done much useful work, sketching the Indian villagers, men, women and children, in various characteristic poses,

each a little cameo of their working life. For she had
discovered that Juan had spoken nothing but the truth
about their industry . . . even small children had tasks
to perform.

She had executed too a rapid impression of Juan
himself, seated on the steer he had brought to its knees.
To be accurate, it should have been an Indian lad she
depicted, but it was as though her pen had a will of its
own and the likeness grew unintentionally beneath her
skilled fingers. This sketch Juan had not seen. She had
wanted to destroy it, but had been unable to bring
herself to do so.

She had come to like and admire Eliseo's simple
villagers, but if she was to fulfil her schedule, she must
move on, from barren, dusty hilltop settlement to
verdant jungle, to ancient ruins; and Eliseo had been
able to tell them of such a city, a day's journey to the
west, set on just such another plateau as the one which
rose behind his village, but a plateau surrounded by
lush, mountain jungle.

'The buildings are mostly covered by the jungle,'
Juan had translated, 'but there are carvings and wall
paintings to be seen.'

At last Juan stopped, pointing ahead of them to a
green mount about twenty feet high, rising out of the
dense growth. Josslyn was aware of unreasonable
disappointment as she, nevertheless, photographed the
eminence. It wasn't an impressive ruin, but, she
reproved herself, she had seen magnificence, impressive
size, good preservation at Uxmal and Chichen Itza. She
moved forward to make a closer examination. The
mound was covered entirely by greenery, but a jutting
piece of masonry proved to be a rough stairway,
ascending to a tower-like structure of crumbling walls.

'I wouldn't trust those steps if I were you!' Juan
warned, but she ignored him. Keeping to her resolution,
she wasn't going to answer him, not even to argue.

It was hardly worth the effort; the view from the top

was of jungle and still more jungle ... monotonous, everlasting green, with no trace of adjoining structures, the remains of which ought to have been visible from above.

Carefully, she began to make her way down; but care was not enough. With six or seven steps left to negotiate, the crumbling masonry began to give way and only Juan's prompt action saved her from a nasty fall. He held her to him ... only for a second, before setting her on her feet, but it was enough to have her stupid pulses racing.

'Not very inspiring, I take it?' Juan voiced her thoughts about the ruin. 'But this is only the start. There should be more further on.'

Further on! Josslyn rubbed a hand across her damp forehead. For a moment she was tempted to sit down, to say she didn't intend to go any further until she had rested. Surely this shaky feeling in her legs must be the effects of her climb? Her near fall? The long trek they had made to reach this spot? Who was she trying to fool? It had been that brief instant when she had been held against Juan's muscular body, reversing all her resolutions concerning him.

Something in Juan's quizzical expression told her that he knew she was flagging and this drove her on, deliberately taking the lead.

It was worth the effort. The jungle opened out quite suddenly into a clearing, in the centre of which was a steep slope ... at its summit a long range of light grey masonry. Sudden elation filled her. She had been right to come here, to see this jungle-embedded ruin in its natural setting, not confining herself to the larger, reclaimed sites.

The horizontal planes of the façade were broken by sprouting trees and spiky agaves, rooted in the walls.

'Oh, Juan! This is tremendous.' In her excitement, she forgot her vow of silence. She circled the crumbling building, but there seemed to be no entrance. Then she saw that Juan was hacking at the undergrowth with an Indian machete ... a fearsome looking instrument, sword shaped and about three foot long. He had removed his shirt and at once Josslyn abandoned her own quest as she stared in fascination at rippling muscles in the tanned back and shoulders, glossed with sweat. She knew a terrible craving to run her hands over that magnificent body, but just then he turned and saw her watching him, gestured impatiently. He had uncovered a small triangular opening ... stone slabs leaning towards each other and wedged by a keystone.

'A Mayan arch,' he told her. 'With care it should just be possible to get inside, but you'd better let me go first, in case of falling masonry.'

Immediately she bristled. He was still making allowances for the fact that she was a woman, something she couldn't tolerate when it related to her work, her undoubted agility. She sighed. Still it was pretty impossible for her to forget *his* sex, though for different reasons. Perhaps that was what impelled her to be wilful, contrary.

'No! It's my expedition. I'll go first,' she told him, shaking off the wistful lethargy the sight of his naked torso had induced. 'Besides ...' a more logical excuse, she triumphed inwardly, 'if any stones do fall, you'll be better at shifting them than I would, if you got trapped.' Without waiting for any further argument, she bent and flashed the torch she carried in her knapsack, peering into the tunnel. It seemed to continue for at least ten feet and beyond there seemed to be some kind of chamber. Her hesitation was only fractional, but Juan noticed.

'Quite sure you want to go in there?'

'Yes. I want to see the carvings and the paintings Eliseo told me about. There ... there won't be any snakes, will there?'

'It's possible!' His tone was challenging her. 'But I've a snake bite kit, just in case you're worried.'

Josslyn took a deep breath; there was something about snakes, even harmless ones, that made her flesh creep, but, summoning all her resolution, she ducked her head and wriggled forward into the hole, her camera digging uncomfortably into her ribs. It was a struggle, but she gained the inner chamber, which she estimated was about eight feet in diameter, maybe seven feet high. Juan had followed close behind her; she had not realised how close, until she turned to speak to him, saying his name, and her arm brushed against his still naked chest. Her fingers encountered his soft body hair, she felt the fine hairs on her forearm rise. It was as though an electric current ran through her, a sharp, tingling sensation. She gasped and hurriedly drew back.

'What is it?'

'N-nothing. You . . . you startled me that's all.'

'You were going to say something?'

'W-was I? I forget. It . . . it couldn't have been anything important.' She turned away and shone her torch around, looking for the promised frescoes.

They were there . . . intricate, painted reliefs depicting ancient gods, beasts and birds . . . and a symbol which appeared frequently, a familiar one, that of the snake with the crest of feathers around its head, a strange mixture of the sacred and the secular. Ancient motifs joined with what she supposed were Christian symbols, yet these too seemed to have a pagan significance, a cruciform shape mounted on the base of a coiled snake. When she queried this with Juan, he confirmed her interpretation.

'You must remember that the original inhabitants of this country were conquered by the Spanish and, though they accepted Christianity, they only chose what suited them and kept what they needed from their own old religions. Mexican Catholicism is a unique blend of two cultures. Even before the Spaniards came, the ancient races had baptism by water, confession, fasting, incense burning and the chastity of priests. Though Catholic saints took over the functions of the old gods, they're still treated much as the idols were. The Indian is superstitious . . . even the patterns he weaves into his clothes are amulets against fate.'

'And the serpent?'

'It doesn't represent the conquest of sin, if that's what you think; it's not the serpent of Eden. It's a retention of the ancient, sacred rattlesnake, a pagan deity of fertility. The Indians revere it above all other gods, because it means the continuation of their race.'

Fertility! The word struck a chord of remembrance.

'Everywhere you go, you'll see one or more of these snakes. In the eyes of the Indians, its power of life and death made it the master of life.'

'This snake cult still exists, doesn't it?' Josslyn thought of the strange ceremony she had seen in the church at Eliseo's village . . . the white clad girls . . . and she shuddered, as the ritual took on a new significance.

'In certain areas, yes. Have you seen enough?' His abrupt change of subject made her curious. It had happened once before and now the two occasions became linked in her mind by a similarity of subject.

'What is the Spanish for snake?' she asked casually, as if the information were of no particular importance to her.

'*La serpiente!*' Again his manner was brusque, but Josslyn scarcely noticed. So Eliseo had referred to serpents . . . but his remark seemed to be addressed to Juan. Given his obvious deference to the younger man, it had most certainly not been intended as an insult. She was curious, but intuitively she knew Juan would not want to be questioned about it.

As she turned to leave the chamber, the light of her torch reflected something green and she bent to pick up a smooth, plump, symmetrical stone. At her delighted exclamation, Juan held out his hand and she almost dropped her find, as his fingers momentarily brushed hers.

'Green jadeite,' he pronounced, 'it would have been used as a chisel.' He was about to return it to her, but,

'No, you keep it for me; you have pockets.' She didn't want to risk another encounter of their fingers.

'It's unusual to find anything at all,' Juan told her. 'The place is grown over now, but down the centuries other people will have come upon it and removed anything of real value.'

'Oh, well. If my photographs of the frescoes are successful, I'll have some unique records to take home.'

Outside once more, she stretched out in a patch of shade and found herself enjoying the sensation of being one of the only two people here in this scene of past history. When she had dreamed of this moment originally, it had been of herself in sole possession of some hitherto undiscovered site, hers alone the find, the pleasure. But she was realising that it was pleasant to have someone to share her enjoyment, someone with whom she could discuss intelligently what she found, what she felt. Someone, moreover, who was knowledge-able enough to explain the significance of the ancient architecture and its decorative symbols.

She was in no hurry to move on, which in itself was unusual. Normally, once she had exhausted the possibilities of a place, she was anxious to be gone, to see fresh sights, reinforcing her own knowledge of herself that a life of travel appealed to her far more than any settled existence. When they'd set out for this ruined village, the ruins had, of course, been only part of its attraction. It had been the journey, too, which was important, the actual fact of travelling, exploring little-known country, observing its flora and fauna, perhaps encountering primitive inhabitants.

Disappointingly they had met no one ... and yet, somehow, the atmosphere of this place held her and she was glad they had it to themselves. The old forgotten settlement beneath the vast, glittering sky, the inter-minable space of surrounding jungle, gave it a feeling of true remoteness, of tranquillity. Did Juan feel it too? she wondered.

'We'd better make camp here,' he said, interrupting her musings; and she realised for the first time that the angle of the sun had changed and shadows had begun to obscure the outlines of the ancient façade. As always, night had come suddenly. In a moment or two there would be black, suffocating, blinding darkness, tropical night replacing the blistering heat of the day.

They certainly would have to make camp. Even if they could have seen to find their way back to the Land Rover, it wasn't wise to drive at night. The fields were unfenced and animals crossing the road were a common hazard even by day.

Josslyn lay on her back beneath the mosquito netting, eyes wide open though she could not see the roof of the tent. It felt strange and very lonely to be in sole possession of their sleeping quarters.

Preparing the evening meal had been her task and it wasn't until the meal was eaten and cleared away that she had gone into the lamplit tent, to discover that only one airbed and one sleeping bag had been set out. For a few moments she had stared down at them in perplexity, before sudden panic seized her. Had Juan suddenly decided that she should, after all, have her own way, be independent of him? Was he planning to return to the Land Rover and ... But no, that was ridiculous. Even he couldn't make that journey back in the dark ... and he couldn't, wouldn't leave her stranded without a vehicle. Nevertheless, she swung round and moved towards him, as he doused the remains of their camp fire.

'Where are *you* sleeping?' Because of her sudden irrational fear, her voice came out shrill, shrewish, and in the light cast by the hurricane lamp he held she saw his eyebrows elevate.

'Since you've seemed so uncomfortable with our

sleeping arrangements these last two nights, I decided I would sleep in there.' He pointed towards the cave-like ruin they had explored.

'But ...'

'Surely you would prefer to have the tent to yourself?' There was a note of mocking surprise in his voice.

'Yes ... yes, of course,' she said stoutly. He needn't think she *wanted* him to share the tent. 'I just wondered ...' and she couldn't prevent the little note of anxiety creeping into her voice, 'whether it would be safe for you to sleep in there?'

'The structure seems pretty sound. I don't think I'm in any danger of being buried alive.'

Josslyn shuddered.

'Don't even joke about it. It ... it's too horrible to contemplate.'

'Would you come to my rescue then, Josslyn?' he asked curiously, moving towards her, looking down at her from his superior height. He reached out and took her hand. 'Would you damage these pretty fingers by tearing at the stones that imprisoned me?'

'Of course I should try.' She attempted to sound matter-of-fact, as casual as he, though her pulses were fluttering erratically. 'As I'd try to rescue anyone in such a situation,' she added quickly, to depress any inflated ideas he might have concerning his importance to her.

'Naturally,' he agreed solemnly. 'I'll say good night then.' He still hadn't released the hand he held and his grasp was so firm that she knew she would not be allowed to remove her fingers from that clasp until he willed it so. 'Are you sure you're not nervous? You're not asking me to move back into the tent after all?'

'Quite sure!' She lifted her chin at him. 'I'm not afraid of sleeping alone. I'd have done that in any case, wouldn't I? ... if I'd been allowed to do as I wished.'

He inclined his head. It was an ironic gesture, but for a moment she felt a great surge of longing within her, as

she mistook the gesture for a preliminary to kissing her;
but with a final pressure of her hand, he turned towards
his choice of sleeping quarters.

The jungle seemed noisier by night than by day, without
another human voice imposed upon its background.
She missed the sound of Juan's steady breathing, the
tangible knowledge of his presence. It had been a
refined kind of torture having him so close. But this
separation was just as painful. She brooded over the
reason for his decision to sleep separately. Had he, too,
disliked sharing a tent? Did he dislike *her*? She had a
feeling sometimes that he disapproved of her. Then,
too, he had certainly been aware of her reactions to
him; he might be avoiding her, since she had made it
quite clear that she did not welcome his advances. She
should be glad, she thought, of the distance he had
imposed between them at this most vulnerable time, the
night, when fatigue relaxed minds and bodies might lose
control over primitive urges.

In spite of a restless night, she woke early to the
ringing chorus of bird song. Something about the
dazzling gold of the Mexican morning seemed to be
tempting her to be up and about, enjoying it before the
full heat of the day. Hastily, she dragged on her clothes
and, moving silently, though it was unlikely that Juan
in his primitive shelter would hear her, she made her
way across the clearing.

Every tree and every bush seemed full of invisible
birds and their chorus of calls, cries, whistles, shrieks,
chattering, or single flute-like notes, accompanied her
long after she left the clearing and followed a path into
the jungle, The undergrowth was not very high, but it
was dense and slung with heavy creepers. Occasionally,
she caught a tantalising glimpse of a tail feather or a
swiftly moving silhouette, but the birds she longed to
see were irritatingly elusive.

The track led to yet another clearing, but here

there were no ancient ruins. Instead, the surrounding
trees were taller, festooned with parasitical plants,
entwined with philodendron ... plants she had only
seen before as cultivated specimens in English drawing rooms. Upper branches of vivid green were
crested with orchids and air plants, some in flower:
pyramids of red and purple, or foaming cream like
sprays that descended as perpetual waterfalls. In the
distance she could hear a continuous murmur that
had nothing to do with the feathered inhabitants of
her surroundings and, beyond the clearing, she found
that the track emerged on to the banks of a bright,
fast-running stream.

Josslyn felt an irresistible urge to immerse her whole
body in the water. It was days since she'd had a proper
shower or a bath and her flesh craved the feel of fresh
cleanliness. Without further ado, she stripped, left her
clothes on a rock and waded into the stream, where she
discovered a pool deep enough to cover her. She
splashed contentedly in the deliciously cold water. It
was peaceful here and yet there was life all around.
Now that she seemed to have become part of the jungle
life, its inhabitants appeared more willing to reveal
themselves to her.

A myriad of butterflies passed in ragged formation; a
kingfisher, a blur of blue and reddish brown, swooped
down over the water, to perch somewhere out of sight;
a pair of brilliantly coloured orioles burst out of the
undergrowth. There were other birds, too, whose names
she did not know ... jet black and scarlet, bright greens
and yellows, jades and chestnuts.

A little too cool now, she waded to the edge of the
stream and sat on the rocks, drying herself in the sun
whose warmth had now penetrated the overhead
canopy. A flight of parrots hurtled by overhead and,
watching them, she did not realise that she herself was
being watched. Absorbed in the jungle and its wildlife,
the almost sensual heat of the sun-warmed rocks lulling

her senses, she hadn't heard the quiet approach of other feet.

'Eve in the garden of Eden!' Juan's quiet drawl brought her head snapping round.

'Well, you must certainly be the serpent then!' she retorted.

What do you mean by that?' His voice was like a whipcrack, but, galvanised by shock and embarrassment that he should see her like this, she had darted back into the water, seeking the sanctuary of the deep pool.

It had been an unwise move; she realised that immediately. It would have been far more sensible to grab her clothes and make for the cover of the undergrowth. Now she was wet again, with no means other than the natural one of drying herself and separated from her clothes by several feet of water ... and Juan's tall, formidable figure.

'Please go away!' It was impossible to sound self-contained and dignified in these circumstances.

'What did you mean by that crack about the serpent?'

'Just what I said. If I'm Eve, you certainly aren't my idea of Adam. That only leaves one other character, except God, and even *you* couldn't be that big-headed. Now will you go away?'

He seemed to relax, he even smiled a little, but he made no move to oblige.

'Don't be so selfish!' To her horror, she saw that he was beginning to undress. 'Why should you have this idyllic spot all to yourself?'

Her eyes followed with fascination the revelation of his naked, virile body.

'You ... you can have it ... you can have it to yourself,' she stammered, 'if you'll just go away while I get dressed.'

'Oh, I wouldn't want to drive you away.' His tone was now that hatefully familiar, mocking one. 'That would be selfish of *me*. Besides, I always think that a pleasure shared is a pleasure doubled, don't you?' As usual, his slow engaging smile seemed to have the power to make her legs wobble and heart leap and he was now totally naked, moving purposefully into the water ... towards her! He moved with a lazy grace that added to his attraction. Never before had she been so conscious of ... actually witnessed ... a man's sexuality.

'Go ... go and find your own pool,' she said faintly. 'There ... there's only room for one here.'

'You *are* selfish,' he said sorrowfully. 'First you want the tent to yourself, and now you won't let me share your bath.'

It was *your* idea to move out of the tent,' she retorted unwisely.

'You mean, I could have stayed? You wouldn't have objected?' He sounded amazed. Oh, he was one hell of an actor.

'I'd accepted the necessity for ... for sharing a tent,' she said stiffly, submerged now, so that only her face rose above water level. 'But this is quite different. We ... we're ...'

'Totally naked!' he finished for her, 'and therefore, you think, more of a temptation to each other than in our circumspect separate sleeping bags?'

'Yes ... I ... I mean ... no ...' Confused and trembling, she looked for a means of escape. There was none. To the side and to the rear was shallow water and he blocked her way. 'I d-don't find you in the least t-tempting, or ... or even attractive.' She was not only stammering with alarm now, but her teeth were also chattering. 'Wh-whatever you're wearing. So k-kindly go away.' She had been in the water too long and she thought wistfully of the sun-baked rocks and her clothes.

A slight frown marred his forehead for a moment.

'I can't believe that you're a woman who is not attracted to men. *Caramba!* I *know* you are not. I have

felt it ... you are all-feminine.' Beneath the water his
hands slipped under her armpits, brushing her breasts
as they did so, and she shivered, tremors that had nothing
to do with the cold water this time, for she knew ... he
had no need to tell her this time ... that he desired her.

She panicked, thrusting with her hands to push him
away, but he was rock-like in his stance and she only
succeeded in losing her own footing, would have fallen
but for his tenacious grasp of her.

'No! Put me down!' She struggled ineffectually as,
effortlessly, he lifted her above water level until she was
exposed to the waist.

'Yes ... all-feminine,' he murmured. 'There *must* have
been men in your life. Yours are not the responses of a
nun. See!' He bent his head and his tongue licked at the
moisture droplets on her breasts, making her quiver at
the pure eroticism of the act.

Squirming in his arms, she endeavoured to cover
herself with her hands, to frustrate the avidity of his
seeking mouth, but he made her hands captive too,
restraining them at her sides.

'Of ... of course there have been men,' she said, and
it was true, but not in the way he meant. 'Dozens of
them, but that doesn't automatically make me a
pushover for *any* man ... or you in particular.'

'And ...' again that puzzled frown of disbelief, '*I*
repulse you?'

'Yes,' she said firmly. 'You're not my type.'

Of course he didn't repulse her. Right at this moment
he was doing exactly the opposite. He was too lethally
male. Even her recent immersion in the water could not
numb the fever heat of her blood, the outrageous
sensations that flooded her body, making her want to
press herself against him; every pulse in her clamoured
to feel against her the naked evidence of his manhood.

She knew as soon as her words were out that it had
been the wrong thing to say; that a man of his blood, of
his arrogance, would never accept any such dictum from

a woman. The closeness she imagined, feared, desired, was thrust upon her as he began to drag her from her refuge and, bending his blond head, closed his mouth over hers with a determined authority that sapped her remaining strength as his body leapt to meet her own.

She kicked with her feet, the only weapons left to her, aiming for his shins, but the silky water effectively cushioned the attempted blows and her movements against him only seemed to spur him on.

His kiss was an intimate one, intimate and deep, his tongue a smooth probe, stroking the inner edges of her lips and, despite herself, she groaned at the exquisite pleasure of it, the responsive sound making his thighs tauten against her, his body, so hard, a heady provocation to senses already aroused.

'I'm going to make love to you, Joss,' he muttered, his teeth tormenting her earlobe.

'No!' Her hands pushed protestingly against his bare chest, but his fevered kisses against the side of her neck were distracting; and she gasped as he nipped the sensitive flesh at the curve of neck and shoulder.

Physically she couldn't fight him, but she could evade his kiss.

'Juan, please, I don't want this. Neither do you. You said yourself, remember? No involvements ... no commitments.'

'This isn't an involvement,' he murmured, his voice roughened, thickened, his mouth seeking to possess hers once more. The softness of his beard against her face had a tantalising eroticism of its own. 'It's physical attraction, Josslyn ... you can't fight that. Why should we deny ourselves the oldest pleasure in the world? We only live once.'

'Because,' she said, surprising herself, for she hadn't realised how deeply ingrained this instinct was, hadn't realised that it even existed within her, 'because I won't give myself physically without commitment ... without love.'

'Then you have loved before?'

She shook her head. 'Not . . . not in the way . . . that way . . .'

'You are telling me you have never given yourself to any man? At twenty-five, you wish me to believe you are still a virgin?' He sounded incredulous. He made it sound the opposite of virtue, she thought, and instead of answering him honestly, truthfully, pride made her retort:

'I'm not telling you anything. It's none of your business. I'm just telling you what I'm *not* going to do now!'

'We shall see!'

She stiffened with alarm, squirmed fruitlessly, as he scooped her up out of the water as easily as if she had been a child, instead of a tall, fully grown woman.

'Put me down!' Her fists beat her protest against his muscular back, yet, in his arms, she knew a mounting wave of excitement, their damp bodies chafing gently together, as he bore her towards the stream's rocky edge.

This was how it must have been before civilisation began, she thought . . . man and woman, unfettered by the restraints of clothing, dwelling in a green, primitive paradise, fulfilling their desires naturally and as often as they pleased, without consciousness of wrong-doing, of the mores of convention or religion; no public opinion thrust upon them.

On the arm that supported her legs, she noticed again the strange, blue marking she had identified, to herself, as an old tattoo. Now that she was so close to Juan, closer than she had ever been before, she could see that it was a birthmark, bluish in colour, unusual in shape. Then, involuntarily, she drew in a breath as she realised what it reminded her of: those carvings, the fanged, feathered, writhing stones; the head of a snake, surmounted by a crest of feathers . . . the plumed serpent! What did it mean?

She was about to question him, but they were on dry land; he was lowering her to the ground, and she knew she had more immediate problems than that of his strange birthmark, its significance . . .

CHAPTER FIVE

THE sun-baked rock was hot and hard against Josslyn's naked body, but Juan's muscled flesh was harder, his lovemaking more heated than the sun's rays, from which his body now sheltered her.

'Juan,' she gasped, 'I . . . I said no. You wouldn't . . . you couldn't be so vile as to force me against my will?'

'It is not against your will, my Joss, your body tells me yes.'

At first he was gentle, persuasive against her continued resistance. Then, as if in sudden anger, his lips probed hers, making them part, a little gasp escaping them, which betrayal of herself brought a greater urgency to the body pressed to hers.

From the moment he had lifted her from the water, carried her to the shore, Josslyn had known exactly what his intentions were and so far she had fought him every inch of the way. She had pleaded with him, appealed to his better nature. That was rich! Juan de Grijalva with a better nature? She had even contemplated insulting him; that had served her purpose before. But now, with his damp warm flesh touching hers, all her weapons were disarmed, resistance forgotten in a strange new clamouring within her that overwhelmed all coherent thought. Her very bones seemed to become limp, making her pliant, so that he was able to mould her to every hard angle of him.

His fingers touched and stroked her sun-warmed skin and it was impossible to conceal from him the shudders of desire that racked her. Almost fiercely, she ran her hands over his bearded cheeks, feeling the soft sensuality of the facial hair against her palms. Then . . . something she had longed to do . . . she pulled his head

down, so that moustache and beard brushed softly
against her breasts, the contact arousing her nipples to
hard, fiery points. It was as though the whole of her
life, her years of determined abstention, the waiting for
she knew not what, had been leading up to this moment
of enticing madness.

Crushed close to him, her lips encountered the male
nipple and, unthinking, she mimicked his own earlier
assault upon hers, feeling his body jerk in response.
Now that her powers of resistance were totally
overcome, she found it easy to make excuses for what
she was about to do. Juan hadn't believed her, but she
had reached the age of twenty-five without experiencing
the total fulfilment of a man's love. If she waited any
longer, perhaps she would never know that fulfilment.
Somehow, she felt that, if she didn't give herself to him
now, she would never in her life give herself to any
other man. This was *the* man ... the vague, uncertain,
shadowy figure, for whom she had held herself
inviolate, not really knowing why she did so, or even
whether this moment would ever come.

He guided her hands over his body and she
trembled with awe at this, her first experience of a
man's smooth-skinned, hard muscled nudity.
Everything about him was sensuous, the strength of
him, his undisguised arousal, his bared legs entwined
with hers.

Wondering at her own daring, she kissed his neck
and shoulders, his hair roughened chest, glorying in his
male beauty ... in the knowledge that she was capable
of making his body shudder and tense with need.
Nothing had ever warned her of her own capability for
sensuality and now she was learning new things about
herself and she was positive, too, that this was right.
This was no furtive assignation, no sordid, secret
meeting in a darkened bedroom, with senses alert for
interruption. This was as God had intended sexual love
should be ... good, clean, wholesome and natural; he

had created this place with just such a coming together in mind.

She had told Juan he was no Adam, but he was ... he was *her* first man.

Yes, it was pagan, it was primitive, but then so was love; it had existed since time immemorial. And so was this country primitive ... the jungle; so, too, were the forebears of this man; and what was she? *She* was her father's daughter ... a free spirit, untied, untrammelled by inhibitions, belonging only to herself and soon, very soon, to Juan. The gift of herself was hers to bestow if she so chose ... and she did choose; every instinct cried out to be made one with him, in the conviction that it could only enrich her ... physically, spiritually, mentally.

In any case, it was too late to turn back now. Juan was holding her as if he would never let her go, the full, lean muscularity of him weighing upon her, his increasingly urgent caresses stirring her to wild, erotic responses she had never imagined possible. Where had she learned such instinctive behaviour? The powerful thrust of him against her brought no fear, only sensations so unbearable that she thought she would die if he did not soon give her release.

His hands moulded her narrow waist, her hips, slid beneath her. His thighs parted hers, bruising the soft inner flesh. Ecstasy flooded her lower limbs; they glowed with a strange, enervating warmth as he sought the pleasure-giving areas of her body. His voice was hoarse as he murmured words she could not understand, but her body responded to their sound rather than to their sense, inviting his penetration. She must learn his language, so that she could understand the endearments he whispered at such moments as these.

A shudder ran through him as, tentatively at first, then with more assurance, she ran exploratory fingers over the hardened evidence of his desire, until one hand enclosed the delicious bulk.

Their coming together was not a submission on her part. They were equals in a glorious mutuality of giving and receiving. After the first initial thrust of pain, her body, though untutored, responded to his with pulsating swiftness, bringing exquisite pleasure to them both ... bringing a new and startling knowledge to her. *She loved him.* This was why, despite her initial resistance, she had finally given way to his ardour, felt no guilt at her submission. This was the meaning of the tensions she had felt in his presence almost from the moment of their first encounter, a tension she had at first mistaken for antagonism, for dislike, had recently come to suspect was more.

'Oh, Juan!' She almost moaned the words against his lips, so spent was she by ecstasy. 'I love you ... I love you ... I'll always love you. I never dreamt it was possible that ...'

'Caramba!' His curse, his sudden withdrawal, interrupted her murmured cries; and at once he ended their intimate closeness, rolling away from her, springing to his feet, striding into the water to immerse himself once more.

Josslyn felt her insides churn painfully. She had expected so much of this time following their first lovemaking. She had expected that he, too, would whisper tender words, cradle her close. Perhaps, after an interval, repeat his possession of her. Every nerve end still quivered for his soothing touch. She had wanted him so much, still wanted the weight of him upon her, his reassurance that she had not disappointed him. A man such as this must have known so many women. The fact did not trouble her; that was in the past. *This* was the present. And the future ...?

He emerged from the water, his naked body magnificent. Moisture coursed down his sinewy thighs, darkening the blond body hair. Now perhaps he would come back to her, say the words she wanted to hear. But he stood over her, his expression harsh, cynical.

'I hurt you, didn't I?' His voice was cold, accusing.

'A . . . a little,' she said shyly, 'but . . . but it doesn't matter. I . . . I know it does sometimes, the . . . the first time. Next time . . .'

'There won't *be* a next time,' he said curtly. 'Get up and get dressed. We're going home.'

At first she didn't understand. Golden eyes wide with incredulity, she stared up at him.

'Why?' she whispered. 'Why? What have I . . .'

'You thought you'd trapped me, didn't you? You thought if you succeeded in making me take your virginity . . .'

'But . . . but you *knew*. I told you . . .'

'I thought I knew, but you were very subtle, Josslyn, very cunning. You purposely misled me, with your hints and innuendoes. I thought you were a woman of experience.'

'I never said . . .'

'But you implied and I took your implication as an invitation. You gave me the impression that you shared my reluctance for emotional involvements. Nothing has changed Josslyn. I won't be . . . *mustn't* be trapped . . . tied down. I did tell you: no entanglements, no "love".'

She studied his cold, handsome face. What a fool she'd been. Nausea welled up in her. What had she done? Thoughtlessly, willingly, she had given herself to him, her heart now, as well as her body . . . gifts that could not be retrieved.

'I . . . I think I h-hate you,' she whispered shakily.

'Hate? Yes . . . well, that's not an unexpected reaction. Carry on hating me, Josslyn . . . far less embarrassing for both of us. And now, we'll strike camp. The sooner I have you back in Mexico City, the better.'

'And . . . and then what?' She felt only a numbness where her heart should have been . . . had been once . . . beating so lustily for him. And he had taken that heart, trampled on it and thrown it back at her, like so much dross. He'd used her, literally, callously, for his own satisfaction. She didn't believe for one moment that he'd thought her to be as experienced as himself. She did hate him now, she assured herself. She had imagined him to be her ideal man. But *he* didn't exist ... not in the personality of Juan de Grijalva. She must hold on to that thought. She didn't love him ... she mustn't love him. But inwardly she wept ... inwardly her craving was as great as ever. But pride came to her aid.

'You won't be embarrassed!' she promised him. 'When we get back to the city, I'll find myself another guide.' She forced her voice to sound as cold and matter-of-fact as his, as she rose to her feet. But she could not stop her hands trembling while she pulled on her clothes.

'You will not find yourself another guide!' he returned fiercely. 'I want you out of this country. You will be on the first plane back to England.' For the first time, his voice faltered a little. 'If ... if there should be ... consequences of ... of this ... this mistake, I will ...'

'*If* there are, and I pray to God there won't be—I wouldn't want to carry anyone of *your* blood inside me— you won't be troubled by it. It's something you'll never know.'

'You'd need help, financial support ...'

'No, I wouldn't!' she emphasised, her golden eyes blazing molten fire. 'I may be inexperienced as an author and illustrator, but I have another career, my art, which gives me a more than comfortable income. I'd die rather than accept anything from you.'

'Because you blame me for this ... this ...' Uncharacteristically, he seemed at a loss for words.

'No!' she corrected him. 'I blame myself ... for my own stupid mistake, my misjudgment of character. I wanted you to make love to me, because I thought I loved you ... thought *you* might come to love *me*. I should have realised, I suppose, that a man of your age, a man who's so successfully escaped all responsibilities, isn't likely to change just because *I* come along. Who or what am I,' she demanded bitterly, 'to affect a stony-hearted monster like Juan de Grijalva? I should have listened to your mother, but I honestly thought I could cope. As for you, you'd better do as your grandmother wishes ... marry Manuela. She looks about as cold-blooded a snake ... as you do!''

For an instant, she thought he would actually inflict physical violence on her, but then he turned on his heel, heading back for their camp site, only turning his head long enough to say roughly,

'Hurry up! We're leaving ... now!'

'I'm glad to see you, of course!' Bridget's welcome was unfeigned, though it was obvious she was puzzled. 'But I must confess I didn't expect you back quite so soon. Is something wrong?' She looked from Josslyn to her son, as though sensing the unusual tension.

'Josslyn is returning to England as soon as she can get a flight.' Juan's voice and face were coldly remote.

Bridget looked even more taken aback.

'You mean, you've got enough material for your book ... already? But I thought ...'

'Things didn't work out quite as she expected ... as either of you expected,' Juan said, before Josslyn could reply, and she knew his words were double-edged, that he was accusing his mother as well as her of scheming. 'Then, too, she's not really suited to roughing it ...'

Oh, how could he tell such lies, when she'd proved beyond any doubt that she was quite capable ... She glared and parted her lips, about to contradict him.

Hastily, Bridget intervened. 'I see!' And Josslyn thought perhaps she did. Bridget had been right about her son's effect on women. Humiliating to have to admit that she, Josslyn, had joined the number of those who'd succumbed to his fatal fascination. 'Well, Juan, your grandmother at least will be pleased. She's been feeling unwell these last few days. Why not go and tell her you're home?'

Josslyn knew very well that Bridget wanted to get her son out of the way, so that she could question her more closely. Juan's mother was very astute; she had realised there was something more than Juan had revealed behind the cutting short of their journey into the interior. That Juan had seen through his mother's ploy was evident too ... but he merely shrugged his shoulders and left the two women together.

'Well, Josslyn?' Bridget turned questioning eyes upon the girl. 'Is it your idea that you should go home? Juan seemed ... angry ...'

Suddenly Josslyn decided to tell her what she wanted to know. After all, why not? It would be a relief to tell someone. Besides, the older woman had already guessed at the truth, so why deny it? She related the happenings of the past few days, leading up to her own unwise admission, but she excluded the fact that she and Juan had actually made love.

'So you see,' she finished, 'I should have taken more notice of your warning. Juan does have a devastating effect on unsuspecting women.' Her voice was bitter and Bridget was sympathetic.

'Josslyn, my dear, I *am* sorry, to be sure I am! It would have pleased me immensely if you and Juan ...' She sighed. 'But there ... I know my son of old. I always knew it would have to be a very special girl to break through his prejudice against marriage, a prejudice I confess I don't understand; but I had hoped *you'd* be the one. Perhaps it's never to be.'

No, there had been no chance of her being the one, Josslyn thought, remembering Juan's only reference to the subject, during the course of their long, silent return to the city. Yet he hadn't been cruel, or scathing, as she would have expected. Instead, his voice had been almost pleading, as though he wanted her to say she understood!

'I don't plan to get married, tied down ... not ever.
I've always felt that way ... at least, since I discovered
... since I was told ... Marriage stops people doing
what they want to do. No, in my case ... what they
have to do.' It was a strange amendment, Josslyn
thought. 'It makes them selfish of their partner,
possessive, jealous of anything and anyone which comes
between them; and especially where I'm concerned ...'
He had been going to add more, obviously, but he
stopped short.

'It wasn't like that with your parents,' Josslyn
couldn't help pointing out.

'They were exceptional,' he retorted, 'and besides, the
circumstances were different ... my father did not
have ...'

'Or with mine!' Josslyn interrupted.

'But your mother wasn't happy about your father's
trips, was she?'

Josslyn couldn't deny it.

'I can't explain, Josslyn, but, believe me, it would be
even more unwise for me to have a wife, than it was for
your father. He didn't ...'

'My father didn't find marriage inconvenient. He
loved my mother!'

'I'm sure he did.' Juan's voice was suddenly gentle,
apologetic? Regretful? 'But it *would* be extremely
inconvenient for me. My wife would have to be an
exceptional woman ... ready to accept ... No, there's
no point in discussing it even. I could not hope for your
understanding. You will just have to believe that for
me, this is not possible.'

'So what will you do now?' Bridget asked, breaking
in on Josslyn's puzzled thoughts. 'Go back to England,
as Juan said?'

'No!' Until this moment, Josslyn had been undecided.
Hurt, mortified and ... she was honest with herself ...
as much in love with Juan as ever, despite his cruel
rejection, she had been almost inclined to do as he said,

to try and forget Mexico ... and him. But her somewhat battered pride was beginning to reassert itself. After all, she still had her work, Many women had been forced to substitute work for married happiness. 'No, I came here to do a job and I intend to finish it. The Mexican "Sketchbook" has to be completed. Apart from the fact that I want to do it in memory of my father, there's been too much money invested in it. Besides, I do have my self-respect. I won't meekly give up and go home, just because Juan's an unfeeling ...' Just in time she remembered she was talking to his mother and bit back the uncomplimentary epithet.

'But how will you manage? Juan will never allow you ...'

'Then he mustn't know!' Josslyn's golden eyes looked directly into Bridget's faded blue ones. 'Do this for me, Bridie ... please? Don't tell him what I plan to do. We'll let him think I'm giving up, but I won't be ...'

For a moment, Bridget hesitated and Josslyn thought she was going to refuse to deceive her son; then, as if she'd made up her mind about something, she nodded decidedly.

'Right! What are your plans?'

'I'm hoping there won't be a vacant seat on an aeroplane for a day or two. In that time, I hope to find another guide ... someone who can speak the Indian dialects.' In her eagerness, she leant forward, her voice rising a little. 'I want to go to the Olmec country. Doña Albina told me a little about it. It sounds fascinating. I think, if I could do that, I *would* have enough for the book ...' Regretfully, she added, 'I had hoped, while I was here, to get permission to do a portrait of your mother-in-law. I *know* she'd make a marvellous subject.'

'You wouldn't fancy painting my ugly old face then,' Bridget said wryly.

'Oh Bridie, dear Bridie, of course I would. But you

have such a lovely, uncomplicated face. There's so much mystery in Doña Albina, such ... such ancient wisdom. But if I had time, I'd paint you too; really I would.'

'I know! I know! Bless you, but I was only teasing.' But Bridget looked thoughtful. 'You're a good artist?'

'Yes! Oh I know that sounds conceited, but it's not really. Portraiture is really my speciality. And I've painted a lot of famous people ... a lot of ordinary folk too ... and I'm really very successful. I don't take any credit for it; it's a gift I was born with, an inheritance from my father, I suppose; but I *can* capture a likeness and ...' she hesitated, fearing to sound ridiculous, 'I know it may sound silly, but, just occasionally, when the sitter has something special about them ... some unusual quality of character ... it comes out in the portrait. I have this feeling now ... a kind of sixth sense is the only way I can describe it ... that it would happen if I painted Doña Albina.'

'Will you leave it to me?' Bridget said slowly. 'I think I may be able to arrange for you to paint my mother-in-law. If I can persuade *her*, and I think I can ... for an old woman she's very vain ... I believe Juan would like a portrait of his grandmother. She's always had a lot of influence with him ... not always for the best, I'm afraid. And who knows? She's ninety-three after all. She may not live much longer; the opportunity might not occur again ... a real artist under our own roof.'

'That would be marvellous!' Impulsively, Josslyn crossed the room and hugged the other woman. 'And while I painted her, I could find out more about the Olmecs and it would give me time too to find a guide. Doña Albina may even know of someone.'

Afterwards, Bridget told Josslyn that Juan had capitulated with a very bad grace; but since she'd taken the precaution of approaching her mother-in-law first, she had scored a tactical advantage. Even Juan would not go against his grandmother's wishes ... and Doña

Albina was almost fierce in her desire to have her likeness captured, not just as a sketch, but as a major portrait in oils on canvas.

Josslyn hadn't come so extensively equipped, but all the materials she required could easily be obtained in the city.

'Juan says you have two weeks,' Bridget reported, 'just until he comes back from New York. He wants you gone before his return. You know,' she added reflectively, ''Tis very strange. I've seen himself sidestep involvements many times before, but I've never known him appear to dislike a girl as thoroughly as he seems to dislike you . . . and you so lovely . . . I've never known him to actually run away either. 'Tis a mystery to me,' she sighed.

Perhaps those other girls hadn't been foolish enough to confess their feelings so completely, Josslyn thought bitterly, or literally thrown themselves at his feet. Obviously, though Juan had not refused the offer of her body, he was embarrassed now . . . despised her for her wanton behaviour.

She knew, from Harry that 'double standards' were quite as rife in Mexico as anywhere else in the world. It was quite acceptable for a man to go to bed with whomever he pleased; it was quite common . . . and a trivial indulgence, even a sign of virility . . . for a married man to have a *casa chica*, a little house where he kept a mistress. But a woman, unless she were a married man's mistress, was expected to remain a virgin until her own marriage, or face indelible disgrace.

The portrait went well. Doña Albina had chosen to wear a simple costume, such as she might have worn before she became the wife of Don Jaime de Grijalva, and nothing could have pleased Josslyn better. The very simplicity of the cotton *huipil* . . . a rectangular dress with openings for head and arms, woven in several colours and simply embroidered . . . gave more

emphasis to the old woman's strong face . . . still oddly
youthful, due to good bone structure and well cared for
skin.

There was an almost ageless look to the Señora's
face, yet the dark, deep-set eyes held all the wisdom of
her years, a wisdom, perhaps, Josslyn felt, that went
back even further than the Señora's own life span,
inherited knowledge . . . race memory? As she studied
her subject, she knew that Doña Albina in return
scrutinised *her* . . . and that scrutiny, at times, made
Josslyn uncomfortable. She felt as though the elderly
woman could see into her thoughts, her heart . . . and
never more so than when the Señora spoke of her
grandson. It was almost, Josslyn mused, as though she
issued a warning, subtler than Bridie's, about the
dangers of becoming involved with Juan.

Mentioning her grandson's regular absences, the
Señora said:

'I would wish to see more of him, of course, but I
realise he must be about his work.' Surely a curiously
Biblical turn of phrase? 'He is not a domesticated man.
He will never be tamed to traditional home life, but I
would not have it so. He does much good work for the
underprivileged, especially those of my race . . . and
other tribes also. Of this I approve.'

From Doña Albina's conversation, it transpired that
Juan's wanderlust was not just in the pursuit of self-
gratification. With his background . . . a degree in
archaeology . . . he was respected as an authority on
many native cultures, but especially those of his own
country. He had been responsible over the years for the
recovery of several valuable archaeological items, now
housed in the city's museums.

'But he *should* marry,' the Señora said. 'His
grandfather would have wished it.' Why not his own
father? 'He should have a consort. The family name
should not be allowed to die with him, or the family's
special gift.' The old lady made their family sound like

royalty, Josslyn reflected, somewhat amused.

'Special gift?' she mumbled, one paintbrush between her teeth, as she worked swiftly and deftly with another.

'That I cannot speak of. It is not a thing to be shared with outsiders.'

With a shrug, Josslyn accepted the implied rebuke. She was curious, naturally, but not enough to risk offending her sitter and perhaps altering the expression she was fast catching ... of arrogance, of racial pride, and of another pride which was hard to define ... a mysterious, almost, perhaps, spiritual pride?

'Tell me something about the Olmecs ... your people,' she invited instead. Unlike some portraitists, she always encouraged her subjects to talk freely. It gave more mobility to their faces, made the capture of character and expression easier. This, fortunately, was a happier choice of subject.

'What is it you wish to know?'

'Anything you want to tell me.'

'Very well. I come from a small settlement, near Laventa. It is jungle country. Once it was composed almost entirely of *heveas* ... rubber-bearing trees. The region is known as *Olman*, country of rubber, from which we take our name. We Olmecs have no Spanish blood!' It was said proudly, even though Doña Albina had, apparently, condescended to marry a Spanish Mexican. 'Four and a half centuries ago, the Conquistadores overran our country. But the homeland of my ancestors was thickly wooded and inaccessible. Our maidens did not breed with *them*!'

'But *you* married Señor de Grijalva?' Josslyn ventured.

A toss of the white head; a knowing pursing of the lips.

'It was ordained ... expected ...' Disappointingly, she did not pursue the subject.

Just a few touches more and the portrait would be finished ... literally, Josslyn thought, as she looked at the animated features on the canvas before her, a 'speaking likeness'. If only the Señora would carry on talking just a little longer. But she found it was unnecessary to prompt the old lady, who, now fairly launched, continued, her English a little accented, but almost impeccable.

'You still wish to visit Olmec country? I tell you there is much to see: the stone giants, great carved heads ... fine examples of our ancient art. This Juan protects, when unscrupulous men would take the pottery and figurines which are our heritage out of this country ... but Juan does not permit.'

'So he doesn't export them himself then, from his antiques shop?' Immediately, Josslyn realised she had said the wrong thing.

'*Caramba*! Foolish girl! Have I not just explained? My grandson would not exploit his own people. The wares he deals in are the "antiques" of other countries ... foreign trash!' Her expression was scornful. 'You do not think the shop is run for his own benefit ... or for ours? The de Grijalvas do not *need* money.' In the jutting arrogance of Doña Albina's more feminine chin, Josslyn could see Juan's proud inheritance. 'Most of his profits go to buy medical supplies: vaccine for the jungle Indians, tribes that were being destroyed by white men's diseases.'

Josslyn had been aware of Juan's interest in and concern for his less fortunate countrymen, but this was a revelation indeed. She stepped back from her easel, flexing cramped shoulders and hands. She had never learnt the art of relaxation while painting; her total being was always intent, her whole energy and concentration poured out into her subject.

'It's finished,' she announced, with a sigh of mingled satisfaction and relief. She knew it was good.

'Finished?' The old lady was tartly incredulous. 'You have painted for four days only. You said two weeks ...'

'No, not exactly. Sometimes it *does* take that long, when the subject is a difficult one, but you've been easy . . . a pleasure to paint.'

'Let me see!' the old autocrat demanded. With surprising agility for her age, she was out of her chair and at Josslyn's side, her shrewd eyes considering the painted likeness. Tensely, Josslyn waited for some comment. When it came it was an unexpected one.

'*Si* . . . you can paint! You have seeing eyes, I think? You have seen my spirit!'

Doña Albina must be very perceptive, Josslyn thought. She had not expected her sitter to see what she herself had already recognised. The old exciting magic had worked, allowing her to penetrate the crusty, arrogant exterior. It *was* as though she had laid bare the Señora's soul, for anyone who had the gift to see . . . but what *had* she painted? To her chagrin, Josslyn was not sure.

'You are good artist,' Doña Albina repeated, 'but you still have far to go. Maybe you never arrive . . .'

'I do realise I'm not the world's greatest portrait artist!' Josslyn retorted, and she *was* modest about her own work, but she couldn't help the note of pique that had crept into her voice at the old lady's comment; but the Señora continued as if there had been no interruption.

'If you wish to see really great art, come with me.'

Intrigued, Josslyn followed Doña Albina into the next room, a bedroom, furnished with large, heavy pieces that left very little space to move between them. On the wall, facing the great carved double bed, which must dwarf the older woman, hung a portrait.

Josslyn gasped. For a moment she had believed the likeness to be of Juan and, as her heart thumped, she felt the treacherous colour flood up into her cheeks, knew that the Senora had observed it. She was nodding.

'Yes, it is remarkable, is it not? A reincarnation! But something not unheard of in Mexico. That is my late husband, Don Jaime, Juan's grandfather.'

Josslyn felt stunned. Were Doña Albina's words to be taken literally? Did she really believe that her husband had been reborn in her grandson? The idea struck Josslyn as ... unhealthy? Was this the root cause of the old woman's possessiveness, her insistence on choosing Juan a bride of her own race, similar to her in appearance?

'And ... and Juan's father?' she asked hastily, to dispel these uncomfortable thoughts.

The Señora shrugged disinterestedly.

'There is a portrait. I believe my daughter-in-law has it. Juan does not resemble his father in the least, but then, looks and talents often pass over a generation ... as the gift has ...'

There was that reference to 'the gift' again. What had Don Jaime de Grijalva possessed that his grandson had inherited ... apart from his blond colouring and startling good looks? Thoughtfully, Josslyn followed the Señora from the bedroom and returned to her easel. She could see the truth of what Doña Albina had said. She still had plenty to learn about the art of characterisation in the face. When she had looked more closely at the unknown artist's interpretation of Don Jaime, she had been aware that, superficially resembling his grandfather, Juan lacked some quality that the painting revealed ... a quality *she* was not clever enough to analyse, but one that filled her with unease. She was glad it was Juan's grandmother she had to deal with now, and not his grandfather.

But although she had perceived the lesson the old woman had pointed, Josslyn was not too dissatisfied with her own work, and all that remained was to add her signature. This she did, then proceeded to clean her brushes.

While she had been engaged on the portrait, Josslyn had been all keyed up, anxious to have the work progress well, to finish it before she lost the mood. Now, with a sense of anti-climax, she realised she had cut short the time of her reprieve. She had no further excuse for staying on in Mexico ... as far as Juan was concerned anyway ... and she had not even broached to Doña Albina the subject of finding an alternative guide, one who would take her to the Olmec area.

'You will paint more of our family!' The Señora's words cut across her thoughts. 'Yes!' raising her hand as though anticipating opposition. '*Yo lo digo* ... I say it is so.'

Josslyn wasn't unwilling. It would give her an excuse to remain longer.

'Who do you want me to paint? Bridie?'

'*Dios*! *She* is not of our family. *She* is European, as you are. No, you will paint Juan, when he returns.' Obviously the Señora had not been told of Josslyn's banishment. '. . . and you will paint Manuela!'

Josslyn had forgotten that Manuela was actually related to Doña Albina. Oh, if only the old lady knew how much she would have enjoyed painting Juan; what a work of love it would have been! She would have been unable though to prevent her feelings for him showing through her work. Anyway, there was no fear of that. Juan himself would never permit it. But Manuela? She had no urge to paint the mestizo girl, no artistic urge that was, but it might serve a useful purpose, be used as a lever to bargain with?

'Does Manuela know the Olmec country at all?' Josslyn asked, as Doña Albina returned to her seat.

'Of course!' scornfully, 'she is of my race, of my village, and some day *she* will be mistress here in my place. For this she has been trained ... educated ... as Don Jaime educated me.'

Josslyn winced, but she persevered with her idea.

'I'll paint Manuela for you, if you'll allow her to act as my guide into Olmec country. Juan can't spare any more time,' she improvised.

'You will paint her because I, Señora de Grijalva-

Lopez, say she must be painted,' Doña Albina declaimed.

But, unlike the Señora's household, Josslyn was not afraid of this diminutive tyrant.

'No!' she said firmly. 'I'll only paint her on the conditions I've stated. Take it or leave it!' She had expected displeasure from the Señora, but instead she thought she saw grudging respect dawn in the dark eyes.

'Very well, I take.' Her hauteur was not diminished, but at least she had conceded. 'You shall have your bargain.'

The second portrait was a very different commission to execute. Bridget had been indignant when she'd heard of the Señora's command, indignant and decidedly disapproving.

'She makes too much of that girl ... and she takes too much upon *herself*. The days when a man's family chose a bride for him are over, and I've told her so. And if it were right, it should be me doing the choosing, not her ... and I'd choose you. I told her that too!' Bridget said triumphantly, as though it was not often she defied her formidable mother-in-law.

Josslyn shrugged. Neither woman would have much effect on Juan, she suspected.

'Doña Albina keeps hinting at a good reason why Manuela should be Juan's wife ... some "secret"?'

Bridget couldn't enlighten her. 'It may have something to do with his work among the tribes. Perhaps she thinks some of the more suspicious and unapproachable among them will be won over, when they see his bride is one of themselves? But it's ridiculous to make such a mystery of it.'

Josslyn was not altogether convinced that Bridie had hit upon the right explanation. When Juan had spoken of his intention of remaining unmarried, he had hinted at things which could not be revealed.

Although Josslyn did not enjoy painting Manuela,

partly because she was a less interesting subject than the
Señora, with less character in her features, partly
because she disliked the girl and felt uneasy in her
presence, the portrait promised to be as striking in its
way as that of Doña Albina. Uncannily, the mestizo
girl's face was coming alive on the canvas, as readily as
that of the other woman. Josslyn could only attribute
this success to the fact that her artistic muse was
working well at present, not because she felt any
empathy with her almost feline subject. There was a
subtle female power inside that slight body. With her
small stature, Manuela should have been insignificant,
but she wasn't.

To Josslyn's surprise, Manuela, uncharacteristically
voluble in her presence, also talked while the work
progressed. But she felt the girl's conversation was
deliberately chosen, her subject the same as that of her
patroness ... Juan ... her tone possessive, insinuative
of unspoken intimacies.

'Juan? He tired of showing you *our* country?'

'You could say that,' Josslyn said shortly, purposely
intent upon her work. Afraid of revealing her feelings,
she didn't want to discuss Juan with Manuela.

'So you wish *me* to take you to my village?' The
dislike between them was certainly mutual and Josslyn
worked swiftly, eagerly, to represent what she saw in
the mestizo girl's face, catching the curl of a lip, the
depth of basilisk eyes.

'I asked Doña Albina if she could spare you ... to
guide me, yes.' It was not pleasant being in a position
where she had to ask favours of this girl.

'What do *you* want of Mexico, of our people? Why
do you not stay in your own land?'

'I have a job to do!'

'And you are not married? You have no husband to
forbid your absence?'

'No!' Josslyn was abrupt with the girl, because she
suspected that Manuela knew very well all there was to

know about her. She suspected, too, that the other girl had deliberately given the conversation this turn. 'In England men don't dictate to their wives.'

'Ah!' It was a purr of satisfaction. 'It would not do then, for you to marry a man of another race!'

'Doña Albina claims to be pure Olmec, yet she married a Spanish Mexican!' Josslyn knew it would have been wiser not to be drawn into discussion, which would only lend colour to Manuela's suspicious jealousy. If only she knew how little cause she had to be jealous! 'And Juan's father married an Irishwoman!'

'Yes!' The toss of Manuela's dark head was contemptuous. 'But he is not tainted by *her* blood. He has inherited the magic of my Señora, the gift of Don Jaime!'

'Magic? Gift!' This was almost the same conversation she had had with Doña Albina. But Manuela seemed to regret having said so much.

'Such knowledge is not for a *gringa*.'

'Then why don't you talk about something else?' Josslyn snapped. 'Tell me about the Olmecs, unless *that*'s too sacred for my foreign ears?'

Manuela shrugged insolently.

'We are an old race, civilised when your ancestors still wore animal skins and painted their faces with vegetable dyes; this the Señora has told me. We worship many gods ... the jaguar, the snake, the rain god, sun god, the earth mother ... all gods and goddesses of fertility that make our race strong ... not like you Christians, who worship one man who allowed himself to be destroyed.'

'Juan is a Christian!' Josslyn couldn't resist saying. 'Do you sneer at *him* for that?'

'*Is* he?' Manuela sounded amused. 'Are you sure, *gringa*? Has he ever said so?'

He hadn't, not in so many words. But he must be ... or surely Bridget would have mentioned it, deplored it?

'We didn't discuss religion ...' she began, intending to add that there had been too many other subjects of mutual interest. Let Manuela be curious for a change, but the other girl was too quick for her.

'No, this I understand. You would have nothing in common to speak of ... *La serpienta plumosa* ... he would not talk of such personal matters to a *gringa*!'

The second portrait was complete and Josslyn felt reasonably pleased with it. Certainly Doña Albina expressed gratification, 'It will hang some day beside the one you shall do of my grandson,' and Josslyn felt that even Manuela thawed a little, looking from the painting to the artist, with awe in her eyes.

'It is witchcraft,' she said, almost with an air of unease. 'You have taken my soul and put it on to your canvas.' Her manner was totally unlike her usual insolent arrogance.

'Rubbish!' Josslyn laughed aloud.

So, below the veneer of civilisation cultivated by Doña Albina for the girl she intended Juan to marry, there still remained the primitive, superstitious Indian. Somehow the realisation was comforting. Primitive Juan's instincts might be, where sex was concerned, but his was an educated, intelligent mind, above superstition. What had he said? 'I believe only what I know to be so.' He and Manuela would be an ill-matched pair.

Her work completed, Josslyn reminded the Señora of her promise, to allow Manuela to be her guide. Doña Albina's rejoinder was startling.

'*Si*, she shall go with you ... and I, too!'

'B-but ...' Josslyn stammered. She *must* have misunderstood. But the regal head with its crown of white hair was nodding determinedly.

'I have a great wish to see again the village of my birth, before I die. Not since my husband died have I been there.'

'It's quite impossible!' Josslyn protested. 'It will be rough going ... a long journey ... tiring. You're ... you're ...' she hesitated to say the words.

'Too old? So? If the journey kills me, let it be so. Always I have expressed a wish for my bones to lie with those of my ancestors.'

'But what on earth will Bridget say?'

'*Dios!* That one has nothing to say to me. *I* am mistress here still ... and mistress still of my own life.'

'And ... and Juan?' Josslyn could just imagine his fury, if anything happened to Doña Albina. He would blame her.

'You think too much of my grandson's opinion.' Were the words double edged or not? Josslyn couldn't be sure. At the mention of Juan's name, the arrogant old face had softened, but the determination in it had not.

'Me, I go! Or *you* do not!'

CHAPTER SIX

THE trip to Laventa took three long days of tiring driving, with two intervening nights of primitive and uncomfortable camping conditions.

Cactus forests and mesquit plains, fascinating at first sight, had become so uniform and unrelieved as to be tedious and Josslyn, driving Juan's Range Rover, was glad when the land began to drop and cacti were replaced by oak woods bearded by Spanish moss.

It was not without some guilt that she had commandeered Juan's vehicle, but with any luck she would have returned from her expedition into Olmec country before he completed his business in New York. Besides, any other kind of transport would have been totally impracticable for the terrain they had to cover since she had to think of the comfort of at least one of her passengers. The aged Doña Albina had not swerved from her determination to accompany Josslyn.

For the most part of their journey, Manuela maintained a sulky silence, broken only by the necessity of giving Josslyn some direction, or in order to make some complaint. It was as if the mestizo girl resented Josslyn's visit to her homeland.

Travelling together, Josslyn discovered, living together in necessarily cramped conditions, certainly gave you an insight into the characters of your companions. While she and Doña Albina endured their discomforts uncomplainingly, Manuela was not the stoical type and several times the old lady issued a sharp reprimand to her young companion.

Another fall in the land level and the inadequate road began to pass through a belt of cloud forest, where giant ferns spreadeagled beneath upright pines. A few more downward twists in the trail and the vegetation became tropical ... forest land of vivid green, looped with creepers and, beyond, the low-lying jungle, a dark, uninviting, almost repellent area, seething with a blood sucking mass of *jejenes* ... tiny, nearly invisible insects that bit like fury, raising red, itching welts.

It was necessary now to drive slowly and with extreme care; one slight deviation to either side of the narrow track might have them bogged down in the treacherous swampland. But, after what seemed like endless, nerve-wracking miles, the way opened out into a clearing ... ahead of them the village they sought, its many stick huts surrounding a sizeable lake, a broad, serpentine shape, the colour of its surface varying from light sapphire over sandy shallows through viridian, to deep, sky-reflecting blue. Beside the lake were beached several canoes; cattle browsed under the thin foliage at the water's edge.

'So now you have your wish,' Doña Albina said, as Josslyn braked and the Range Rover jerked to a halt. 'You meet my people.' It was said proudly, arrogantly, but Josslyn viewed their reception committee with some doubt.

Two men approached their vehicle, their initial manner strutting, aggressive. They had plump, round faces, their noses were broad and negroid. Straight, blue black hair grew out from their large heads in a rough thatch. Thick necks scarcely showed the division between face and heavy bodies, with bellies that overhung their tattered cotton pants, their only garment. Could the delicate featured Señora and Manuela really spring from the same race? In rough tones they seemed to be questioning, almost threatening the three women.

But Doña Albina treated them with hauteur as servants, members of the inferior tribe it seemed they were, speaking to them in a rapid almost fluting dialect. At once the men were all subservience, their manner and mien rapidly altering, as they almost grovelled before the old lady.

Now a crowd of women and children appeared, tall, long-skirted women, rather handsome, their full cheeks tapering to narrow chins, the children lurking behind them; all ... boy or girl, Josslyn couldn't be sure which ... had black hair that hung over bright inquisitive eyes and covered their shoulders.

These escorted them towards a hut larger than the rest, from which emerged a man, who had obviously been warned of the visitors' arrival.

Imposingly tall, ascetic looking, Xchemax was evidently of the first importance. His hair was like that of black, gleaming feathers. His luminous, smoke-grey eyes under black lashes set in a dark, warm bronze skin, seemed to assess Josslyn and Manuela in turn, while Doña Albina spoke ... as to an equal now, despite the man's youth. She was obviously explaining their presence and Josslyn could not be sure, but she thought she heard Xchemax repeat several times a word she had heard before ... 'Itzpapalotl'; and from the glances in her direction, gained the distinct impression that he spoke of *her*! and that he and the Señora were in conflict, outright disagreement. But at last the Señora turned to Josslyn.

'You will be offered every courtesy, every co-operation, on the understanding that you do not try to introduce outside ways or customs to the villagers, or attempt to lead others here to corrupt and destroy their ways.'

Josslyn promised readily, but something puzzled her nevertheless and she expressed her curiosity frankly.

'If your tribe are so insular, so much against change, how was it you were allowed to leave, to marry an outsider? And what about Manuela?'

'I was permitted to leave for reasons that you could not understand ... religious reasons,' Doña Albina told her a trifle loftily. 'My marriage with Don Jaime was foretold at my birth, preordained ... and Juan follows in his footsteps.'

With Manuela as *his* foretold wife? Josslyn wondered, but could not bring herself to ask, especially with the mestizo girl listening, a scornful expression on her haughty little face.

The events of the next few days fulfilled all Josslyn's expectations. There was material here and to spare. If she wished to do so, an entire book could have been devoted to the Olmecs, their history, culture and strange customs. At Xchemax's command, she was guided to nearby ruins ... a rectangular, stone fort with crumbling walls and a tower twenty feet high; she was shown *muñecos* ... terracotta figures discovered in what were probably ancient burial mounds. Her hours were rapidly filled as she made lightning sketches of the villagers about their everyday tasks. The women still practised the pre-Hispanic traditions of textile design and manufacture. Spinning and weaving techniques had changed little since ancient times, the cotton thread or *henequen* fibre still being spun on a hand spindle. Other women knelt at the waist loom or *otate*, patiently weaving lengths of cloth for family use.

But, source of much interest, absorbing, though frightening too, was the dwelling of the *curandera*, the village wise-woman or witch. Here were a collection of objects, some fascinating, some decorative, others sinister ... racoon tails; stuffed birds, strings of them; skins of boa and rattlesnakes. Crude pots contained herbs, corpses of toads, polished beans ... an assortment of amulets.

But if the villagers held the *curandera* in awe, it was evident that the wise-woman herself regarded Doña Albina with a far greater respect and that Doña Albina expected and accepted it as her right.

The days held their quota of interest, but it was at night that Laventa seemed to come alive, in a way that Josslyn found both stimulating, yet a little frightening in its dark, pulsating energy. It was a strange darkness, the Mexican darkness. The heat, the blackness seemed to oppress her on all sides. Strange emotions conflicted within her and she found herself wishing Juan were here to share her experiences of this primeval world, his own enthusiasm bringing the place, the sense of discovery and adventure more alive for her, as it had done on other occasions.

Dispersed about their various tasks by day, by night the community came together as a whole, around an immense fire, constructed near to the lakeside. In this atmosphere, stories were told and songs sung, religious or mythical in origin.

Surprisingly, it was not Manuela, but Doña Albina who translated their meanings for Josslyn, explained their significance ... a Doña Albina who had shed with her European clothes some of her civilisation. Here she wore a woven, red fringed cloak-like garment, its design incorporating, among black and red zigzags, a bird and a snake. The colours red and black, Manuela told Josslyn in one of her rare moods of communication, were indicative of wisdom, red being the greater wisdom.

Music, Doña Albina told the fascinated girl, was divine in origin, a gift from the god-king, Quetzalcoatl. Never performed for art's sake, music and dance were always part of religious rites ... more pagan than Christian, Josslyn suspected. These ritual chants were accompanied by instruments as old as the melodies themselves: the windy tones of the *chirimia*, the trumpeting notes of the conch shell, the sonorous drumming of the *huehuetl*; gourd rattles clattered, bells of wood and hide rang. The music had a timeless, primeval quality, intense and passionate. The men of the tribe, half naked, danced in a circle, their singing full throated, yet with a note of sadness and yearning caused by the voice slowly dropping at the end of the phrases. The sound filled Josslyn with strange, formless, primitive longings. The chants expressed the Olmecs' worship of the spirits of the waters, into which they threw little images and idols made of baked clay.

'It is from the lake,' Doña Albina had told Josslyn in all seriousness, 'that the old gods of Mexico re-emerge ... but not, alas, in every generation. Sometimes many hundreds of years may pass before there comes a reincarnation. So, when the fishermen take their canoes upon the lake, they must always make tribute to the gods, a gift of propitiation, of entreaty, that this time *He* will not be taken from them.'

A gift of propitiation? A prayer that their god would not be taken from them? Which god? For she could not believe it was a Christian god of whom the Señora spoke. Josslyn understood none of it. Mexico was as fascinating and mysterious as she had expected, but infuriatingly impenetrable. It seemed to her that its people held back something of themselves, that deeper essence for which she was seeking, without which her work would lack completeness.

'What form does the gift take?' she questioned Manuela when, for once, the elderly Señora de Grijalva was not there to answer her questions. She recalled what she had learned about the Aztec holocausts in which as many as 20,000 victims were immolated at a time. 'I suppose in former times it would have been a human sacrifice?'

Manuela smiled. It was an inscrutable movement of her face.

'What makes you think our customs have changed at all?' she asked. 'The Olmecs are great magicians ... death has great power ...'

'Oh, but surely ...' Josslyn stopped, looking doubtfully at Manuela. At first she had believed the mestizo girl must be joking, but suddenly she was not so certain. Manuela had never before shown any vestiges of a sense of humour.

*   *   *

With sufficient material in her sketchbook, enough for several books, Josslyn was ready to make the return journey to Mexico City, before Juan could discover her unscheduled absence. But fate, or perhaps Nature, in the shape of the weather, was against her. The night before her planned departure, a spectacular storm, lasting several hours, clapped down upon the village, the violent glare of the lightning illuminating the settlement for minutes at a stretch; the rainfall was massive, reducing the swampland to an impenetrable morass, the tracks indistinguishable from the ground on either side.

When it rained in Mexico, Josslyn thought ruefully, it certainly put heart and soul into it. The torrential rain just fell down, bringing twigs and even whole branches from the the trees, and she cringed in the hut she had been allocated, longing for the night to be over. Somehow a storm seemed far worse at night and she could not help thinking of that other storm, much briefer than this, which had isolated her and Juan in the arbour up on the *azotea*, of her physical response to him then . . . and since; and despite the fact that she knew there was no future for her with Juan . . . he had said so . . . foolishly she longed now for the safe haven of his arms against the elements.

But the passing of the storm, the coming of morning, brought no comfort either, for with the reappearance of the sun came retribution, in the shape of the very man for whom, last night, she had longed . . . Juan de Grijalva.

It was the sound of voices raised in shrill surprise that brought her from the hut, to see almost the entire population of Laventa gazing skywards, every face expressing superstitious awé or trepidation. The sight which so excited them was not a strange one to Josslyn, but it was obvious that a helicopter was new in the experience of the Olmecs. Its shining metal body reflecting the sunlight, it descended lower and lower, until at last it landed in the clearing, the disturbance

caused by its rotating blades causing the onlookers to
run for cover.

But with the cessation of mechanical movement and
the emergence from the belly of this strange bird of a
single, bush-clad figure, the villagers' courage swiftly
returned. They were eager now, excited, as they, too,
recognised the new arrival. Gestures, attitudes of
abasement, lined Juan's path from the helicopter to
where Josslyn stood. Among the crowd only she, Doña
Albina and Manuela remained totally erect.

With only a brief acknowledgment of the murmuring
villagers, Juan made straight for the three women, his
stride forceful, impatient; and as he drew closer, Josslyn
could see that he was angry . . . furiously angry. Despite
her determination not to flinch before his rage, she felt
the grip of a strange apprehension. In his towering
anger, he was the ultimate in masculinity, striking that
old, primitive chord of attraction within her. She parted
her lips, intending to be the first to speak, to show him
that she was fearless before his premeditated aggression,
but he forestalled her. She knew again the tingling
sensation of his calloused palm against her skin, as he
seized her arm in a steely grip.

'What the hell do you think you're doing? I return
home to find that not only have you purloined my
vehicle, taken off on a dangerous, foolhardy journey,
but that you've also dragged along a frail old lady,
presumably to act as your guide.'

She was too angry to deny this latter accusation . . .
that could wait. Instead as he shook her arm, his
strength causing her to stumble, she flared up at him.

'Don't try and push *me* around!'

'That's just what I do intend to do!' His voice was
not an enraged roar, but the cold cut of steel, infinitely
more effective. 'You're obstinate, wilful. You need a
man's hand upon you.'

Not just your hand, her body cried out yearningly,
quivering at his touch, remembering how once the

whole of their flesh had touched at every point. Not just your hand, but all of you. Yet while her body made its plea, her golden eyes flashed defiance.

'You have no right to order or direct my affairs. I'm my own mistress . . .'

'But you have also been *mine* . . . once . . .' he muttered, jerking her close to him, so that his words were for her ears alone and she knew the familiar warmth in her loins, generating sexual fantasy, her legs weakening, as if that growing heat invading her also melted her bones.

'*Once*!' she hissed back at him, refusing to allow her limpness to reveal itself to him. 'But never again . . . never. You yourself made that quite clear.'

'I *could* change my mind!' To outward appearances his features were still cold and austere; only Josslyn knew of the heat of his flesh, turning her own to an answering fire.

'But *I* shan't change *mine*!' she retorted and only wished she could guarantee her own strength in that respect.

'We have to talk!' he said curtly. 'This minute . . . alone!'

Adamantly, she shook her head.

'We have nothing to talk about, you and I. If it hadn't been for the storm I would have been on my way back to Mexico City by now.'

Despite her protests, inexorably he was drawing her apart, towards the edge of the lake.

'Are you sure of that?' Words and tone were sceptical, then became urgent. 'Would to God that you *were* safely back in the city. What possessed you to come here, to Xchemax's village, without my protection? Don't you realise it isn't safe?'

Proudly, she lifted her chin.

'Our association was over . . . our *business* association,' she stressed, 'and I don't need your protection. I never have. Besides, I'm here with your grandmother and Manuela. Xchemax seems to hold them both in great respect, so why should he harm *me*?'

'Little fool! Manuela and my grandmother are of his race ... Xchemax is my cousin; but in beliefs we are far apart. I have received the benefits of having a European mother, an education ... of civilisation. *He* has never left his native village. His loyalties lie with the old gods, the old religion, and if something were demanded of him, in the name of those loyalties, he would perform it unquestioningly.'

'What could be asked of him that could concern me?' Josslyn asked scornfully.

'Perhaps your death.' His reply was given so sombrely that she could not doubt that he believed what he said and for a moment she was startled into silence. Then, shakily, but with an attempt at scornful laughter,

'I ... I don't believe you. For some reason of your own, you're trying to frighten me.'

The handsome head moved in a gesture of negation.

'I've no wish to frighten you, only to protect you, if I can. For the future, until we can leave this place, you'll stay close to my side ... by day and ...' he paused, then, significantly, 'by night.'

Josslyn stared at him, aghast at the implication of his words. She didn't know whether to believe him or not; was this some devious plan of his? And if she were to believe him, why should Juan be concerned about her safety? She meant nothing to him, apart from the fact that she was a woman who had provided him with a momentary gratification of his physical senses. It could be some chivalrous loyalty, she supposed, arising from that fact. But that was not what she wanted of him.

'In that case,' she retorted, 'we'll leave now.' She had no intention of spending the night time hours in his company. She knew too well the temptations and tortures such a hazardous undertaking could bring in its wake.

'Impossible!' he said curtly. 'It would be extremely discourteous in me to leave so soon after arrival.' Then he added, puzzling Josslyn, 'And it might lead to misunderstanding. Xchemax's people might think I'm displeased with them.' Before she could ask him to clarify this remark, he was propelling her back towards the place where Xchemax stood, addressing the chief in his own language, translating briefly for Josslyn's benefit. 'I've explained that I will share *your* accommodation.' He spoke quite openly before Doña Albina and Manuela and as Josslyn gasped a protest, she looked nervously in their direction.

There was no mistaking the disapproval in the older woman's face, but Manuela's expression was the harder to read and therefore the more disturbing. Yet neither woman gave voice to their feelings ... unusual, surely?

Equally disconcerting to Josslyn was the knowledge that the remainder of the day still stretched before her, hours in which to anticipate and dread the coming night.

Recovered from the fear aroused by his unexpected means of arrival, there was no doubt that Xchemax's people welcomed Juan's presence. The bolder ones among them ventured close to the gleaming helicopter, stroking its shiny surfaces with tentative, exploring fingers.

Josslyn was beginning, through Doña Albina's constant translations, to understand a little of their tongue and she recognised such phrases as 'flying snake', 'the feathered serpent', and presumed that such terms were all their limited knowledge of the outside world, their very basic vocabulary, could conceive of to describe the machine.

One thing she soon discovered was that Juan had meant his words quite literally, that she should remain constantly at his side.

'Come with me,' he ordered and, unable to think of a reasonable excuse to refuse his company in daylight, she permitted herself to be steered towards the swampy edge of the lake, where the canoes were moored. 'Xchemax has ordered an expedition, as . . . as a kind of entertainment.'

'For you?'

'For me,' he agreed.

There was no doubt that Juan was an honoured guest . . . as Dona Albina's grandson no doubt and, of course, as Xchemax's cousin.

'A fishing trip?' she hazarded and was horrified by his casual reply.

'We go to look for alligators.'

'But . . . but isn't that dangerous? I . . . I'd no idea there were alligators. I . . . I'd been thinking of swimming.'

'Just as well you didn't,' Juan said sharply. 'The sacred lake is not for swimming. It would have been viewed as sacrilege. These are a very religious people.'

'Religious!' she retorted. 'I'd call it superstitious! Sacred lake . . . whatever next?'

'Take care you don't find out,' was his somewhat ambiguous reply. 'Anyway, if you want somewhere to swim, I'll show you a safe place tomorrow.'

'Can't we leave tomorrow?' she almost pleaded, as Juan pulled one of the canoes closer to the bank. 'I've finished my work here. I want to get back to England.'

'But *my* work isn't finished,' he said obscurely. 'It will be several days before we can leave. Now please get in, without any further delay. You're holding everyone up.'

A long line of canoes drifted away from the bank; they were all long, narrow dug-outs. Juan had directed her to a place three feet from the stern, placing himself just behind her, so that she was electrically aware of his legs straddling her hips. They glided across a clear stretch of water at the narrowest point of the lake, entering a tunnel which opened into the mangroves on the other side. In spite of the climate, the enclosed air was so cold that Josslyn shivered, a shiver which she swiftly repressed, not wishing Juan to misinterpret its cause. She was humiliatingly aware that he knew only too well the physical effect he could have upon her.

Around them, the stems of the mangroves rose in a dense tangle, through which little light was able to filter. It was, she thought with a sense of rising hysteria, a parody of a fairground tunnel of love ... with the thought of alligator at its end making it a house of horror.

A sudden thought had her turning her head towards Juan, then swiftly away again as she found his bearded face so close to hers; and when she spoke it was with downbent head, her voice muffled, yet fearful.

'Y-you won't have to ... to kill an alligator, will you?'

'Kill an alligator? My dear Josslyn ...' His voice was lightly, irritatingly amused. 'I presume your foolish words are prompted by some misguided fear for my safety ... I'm flattered. But this is no alligator hunt. It is a pilgrimage rather, to one of the gods of the water and swampland. The Olmecs would no more think of killing an alligator than they would think of killing my grandmother or myself.'

Feeling foolish, humiliated and wishing she had never expressed her dread, Josslyn tried to concentrate on her surroundings. The swamp, though eerie, was not silent, but alive with the calls of unseen birds, as they twisted and turned through increasingly narrow tunnels of yellow water, the flotilla of canoes nose to tail. Then Juan, in the leading canoe, ceased his stroke, the boat, without propulsion, almost stationary. Over Josslyn's shoulder, his hand, with finger extended, indicated a muddy bank only a few feet away; and she could just make out a long, dark object lying half submerged in the water.

Juan's movement had brought his body closer to hers; she could feel the steady stream of his breath against her cheek and she felt an insane longing to lean back against him, to turn her face up to his in a shameless invitation of his kiss. Only the knowledge of the following canoes prevented this total abasement of her pride and she held herself all the more erect as they continued on their gliding journey; but it was a warning of what she must endure, until Juan decreed that they return to civilisation.

Glancing back, she saw that each canoe, as it passed the recumbent monster, flung some tribute towards its muddy resting place ... raw meat! ... and with a thrill of horror she saw the creature stir, larger now that its body was fully exposed, before it slipped into the water to retrieve its booty. She could no longer doubt the tribe's adulation of the beast they looked upon as a god.

So passed the morning. The afternoon swooned in sultry silence. Then came evening.

If the morning's excursion had been in Juan's honour, there was no doubt that the evening's events were similarly intended. Again the lakeside bonfire was lit, again the drums and cacophony of other instruments vibrated on the thick blackness of the night air ... a savage melody. The drum was a slow, regular vibration, calling to Josslyn's blood like a great heartbeat, deepening the thud of her own, conscious as she was of Juan's nearness, only his dark profile visible in the light of the fire; but his arm, his thigh, pressed to hers, as they sat, part of the circle of onlookers, waiting for the dance to begin.

Apart from the music, the night seemed to have gone still, enclosing them in an other-worldliness that bore no relation to reality.

The dancers, with their black heads, their powerful, handsome, naked torsos, both attracted and repelled Josslyn, so open were her senses at that moment to masculine physicality. The glistening male bodies recalled for her that moment when Juan, the water draining from his bronzed frame, had carried her to a water's edge and made her his, irrevocably, though he had afterwards denied the permanence of his possession.

Mexico had brought her to a full realisation of life ... Mexico, and Juan. Here only, it seemed to her, did her life burn with colour, with the fire of purpose. Her former, remembered life seemed pallid and sterile by comparison.

Softly, slowly, one after another, the men began to dance ... not the wild, joyous leaping Josslyn had seen on other evenings, but a slow, heavy, ritualistic step, a curious bird-like tread, until all were slowly revolving about the fire and all the while the drum echoed the beat of a heart.

Despite the slow, deliberate movements, like those of predatory birds seeking their prey, the dance held an undercurrent of excitement, of sensuality, that communicated itself to Josslyn, as though, she thought, all her senses were more aware, more alive than they had ever been before, so that she was not really surprised when a man broke away from the circle, approached a seated girl, waited before her in silent invitation. Josslyn found herself holding her breath. Would the girl accept? She did. Shyly, with downcast eyes, she rose, took the man's hand and was led back into the circle around the fire and this time, clasped in each others arms, they trod the soft, sensuous, heavy dance step. Now all the men chose partners and a sudden movement at her side told Josslyn that Juan intended to take part. Who would he take for his partner? Manuela?

But he was standing before *her*, the dancing firelight making his face look as though he smiled slightly.

'Come, *querida*!' It was a command, the words softly, magnetically spoken, and, mesmerised, Josslyn rose, took slow, reluctant steps forward into his arms. But once there, all reluctance fled. This was where she belonged.

In the moving circle, he held her with a hard, barbaric nearness, as, awkwardly, she tried to follow the dance steps. But soon she was only aware of the slow, pulsing pendulum of his swaying body, of his nearness that transcended all other considerations.

A shy, sideways glance at other couples, showed them similarly absorbed, the absorption of man with woman, woman with man ... the absorption with sex. Josslyn had never been more conscious of herself as a woman, caught up in the maleness of her partner, whirled in the slowly revolving ocean of desire.

Guided at first by Juan, her feet seemed soon, of their own volition, to follow the convolutions of the dance. Unconsciously she relaxed, letting her soft weight lie loosely against his strong, erect body. Time seemed to stand still, as the dance moved slowly onward, around and around the great fire.

A tiny corner of her mind told her that this was not dancing, it was sexual in origin ... it was blatant lovemaking. Juan's breath fanned her temple, his fingers explored her spine, the rounded curves of her buttocks, with a growing intensity ... a possessiveness.

She looked up for an instant, contemplating protest, but the fire-glitter in his eyes showed a raw desire that made her breath catch in her throat. Then he pulled her closer, his hands fast upon her hips, his legs spreading astride as they swayed in time with the drum beat ... as he deliberately allowed her to recognise the primitive thrust of his arousal.

Her mind swam, the blankness of heady forgetfulness blotting out that earlier humiliation when he had rejected her words of love. Inhibitions melted, she knew a longing to give and to receive, to satiate the longings he openly displayed, even as she craved the satiation of her own mounting need.

Somewhere in the growing crowd of swaying bodies, a voice was raised in song, a song taken up by other lips.

'The god who hid his face came out of the water
The dark sun meets the day sun.

Without each other they are nothing.
His bride says to herself: this is Quetzalcoatl,
My lord, my master. My white breast tips are his.
He is mine to hold ... I ... Itzpapalotl ...'

'What does it mean?' Josslyn lifted her face to ask and felt Juan's lips brush hers before he answered.

'Something and nothing, yet everything to them. They sing of their god, the god of life and death, of fertility ... his coming together with his bride ... the earth mother. ...' He hesitated, then, 'Their song is for us, too, Josslyn.'

She didn't understand. What had the Olmecs' ritual chants to do with her and Juan?

'The song tells of marriage, of the mating of twin souls ...' Abruptly, 'Josslyn, I've told Xchemax that you will be my wife.'

'You ... you *did what?*' Josslyn's words came faintly and for the first time in their acquaintance, his eyes did not meet hers directly.

'I had reason to believe that you wouldn't be adverse to the idea ...'

Josslyn went hot with embarrassment. He was referring to her unguarded outburst, when she had believed, so briefly, that he had ... despite his declared intentions to the contrary ... fallen in love with her.

'I ... I made a mistake ... I ...'

She was interrupted as the music began again; but this time the drum had a strange, inward pulse that induced an answering response within her, a deep stirring of feeling.

The Indians had moved around them in a silent circle, watchful, waiting, Xchemax among them.

'They wish the ceremony to take place here, in the village of my ancestors.'

This was ridiculous. It couldn't be happening to her. It was like a dream, unreal. Juan couldn't seriously mean ...

In high, remõte notes, a lone singer took up the
theme of the music, music like no other Josslyn had
ever heard . . . a far-off cry on the night air. It conjured
up the mists of time, of love and lovers from time
immemorial. It pierced one to the heart, carrying with
its arrow-like shaft a sense of predestination, a message
of the uselessness of resistance.

'Drink of my strength, of my potency . . .' sang the
voice . . . and, simultaneously, a gourd was handed to
her.

'You must drink,' Juan told her. 'It is the custom.
They will be offended if you do not.'

She drained the draught; it was a bitter one and she
had much ado to hide her moue of disgust. Juan's hand
stroked her hip and she began to tremble; she had no
strength against the potency of him. Like the molten
wax of a candle she bent to his burning flame.

'Well?' he asked softly, insistently.

She tried to meet his gaze with defiance, to refuse,
but in the firelight his eyes flashed uncannily,
primitively compelling.

'You *can't* be serious,' she whispered. 'There's no
priest here, no . . .'

'Xchemax is both chief and priest of his tribe.'

She recovered a little of her strength, the sanity that
his touch seemed to dispel.

'Don't be ridiculous,' she snapped. 'Even if I were to
agree . . . and I don't . . . how could we be married by
some primitive native ritual? We're both Christians. At
least I am . . . though I'm beginning to have my doubts
about you . . .'

'Does it matter?' His voice was soft, husky, enticing,
as was the pressure of his body. 'In everything but name
you are already mine. If you wish, another ceremony, a
civic one, can be performed when we get back to
Mexico City.'

'But *why* should you marry me? You don't want to
be married. All along you've stressed it . . . "no

involvements". What has changed?' Her mouth was dry, the bitter aftertaste of the draught she'd drunk. She felt confused.

'Too much to be explained now. We have no time. Humour the beliefs of my grandmother's people, Josslyn? Hmm? What harm can it do, after all?'

What harm indeed? she found herself thinking. Obviously, for some reason, Juan wished to please Xchemax and his tribe. Of course there was no question of the later civic ceremony he had mentioned. He didn't really want to marry her, only to placate this weird intensity of feeling to which the Olmecs had aroused themselves . . . and her, she admitted. After all, there was no reason why she shouldn't co-operate, partake in their quaint ritual. It meant nothing to her, bound her to nothing, and Juan knew that, too. He was no primitive savage.

On the point of capitulation, she was aware of the women of the tribe moving about her. One knelt to remove her shoes, so that Josslyn stood barefoot on the still warm earth. Another performed the same service for Juan. A brilliant scarlet and black *serape* was placed about her shoulders, a blue and white one about Juan's.

'Wedding garments,' he said. Again the cup was offered to her and this time she downed its contents quickly, as one would an unpleasant medicine. Then Juan led her, still half-reluctant, to where Xchemax stood, a tall, awe-inspiring figure in a pure white *serape*, and somehow Josslyn found that they were kneeling before the Amerindian chief, his hands stretched above their heads. He spoke slowly, impressively, in his own langugage and in an undertone; Juan translated.

'Barefoot on the living earth
between night and day,
man and woman,
god and goddess,
be perfect in one another.

To the woman, the man is rain from heaven.
To the man she is the fruitful earth.
The man, Quetzalcoatl, kisses the breasts of the
    woman, Itzpapalotl.
In the heart of the night, woman meets man
    and does not deny him.'

Her brain felt dulled, the strange hypnotic words filled it; her body was still fevered by the passions of the dance; she was a passive participant. Then it was over and she and Juan were walking, closely entwined, towards the hut that was hers; and all at once she realised the destiny towards which she was moving. Somewhere, dimly, the thought came to her that she should be holding back, yet it was physically, mentally impossible to do so and he was sweeping her inexorably onward, half carrying her, brushing aside the rough fringed, curtaining grasses of the doorway, turning her into his arms, as the small hut enveloped them in its dark intimacy.

'Josslyn!' His voice was rife with sensuality as with increasing urgency his hands caressed her spine, urging her closer, grinding her hips against his in an impossible endeavour to join her body totally with his. His mouth covered lips that could only murmur faint sounds, which blurred into groans of invitation. His tongue slid in and out repeatedly, in an invitation to deeper intimacies.

He drew her down on to the straw covering of the floor, all that constituted the Olmecs' conception of a resting place, and she felt her body being explored by strong, hard fingers, with a freedom she had no will to resist. When he touched her caressingly, all her body flowered. Juan became her universe; he filled her body and soul with a completion, the power of which was greater than her own will. He had made her his before and since then her body had cried out for him to reassert his ownership. He had promised, hadn't he, she remembered dimly, that that bizarre ceremony had only been the prelude to conventional marriage? So why deny him and, in so doing, deny herself what she most craved?

She helped him to remove the simple garments they wore, pressed her mouth against his jawline, loving the feel of the blond silk against her lips, felt the flower of her femaleness opening to him, his masculinity diffusing into and throughout her, as they rose in a heady welter of sensation to the all transcendent moment of physical ecstasy; and Josslyn, all reasoned drowned in sensation, allowed herself to believe, to entertain the lovely world of elusive make-believe where now everything was possible, even that Juan had possessed her this time in love.

A fool . . . in a fool's paradise.

CHAPTER SEVEN

WHEN she woke, head throbbing, mouth dry, he had gone. Last night she had looked forward to waking in his arms, waking to tender words ... even to renewed lovemaking. But the place where he had lain beside her was cold and empty and she, too, felt suddenly so. She'd been a fool last night to give in to the urges of her body. How did she know she could trust his promises?

She rose to her feet and restlessly paced the hut, filled with self-doubt, self-contempt. She should have kept to her very first resolution when, right from their early acquaintance, she'd tried to see Juan merely as her guide, a necessary evil, to be ignored as much as possible. But it had been impossible to ignore him in the physical sense.

In the cold light of day, she knew that last night's waking dreams had been self-delusion. Nothing had changed. How could it have done? Juan didn't love her but, his passions inflamed, as hers had been, by the heady ritual, he had wanted her. She didn't have Juan's heart; all she had was an obsession that was a pain and a longing for something that didn't exist, except in her own imagination.

Totally, she discounted last night's 'wedding cere-mony' ... a superstitious rite that might be sufficient for this ignorant, superstitious tribe; but she was no untutored native ... and neither was Juan! He could not possibly believe in all that mumbo jumbo. And she? She had allowed the fever of the dance, the mystery of the Mexican night to sway her senses, to overpersuade herself into a coupling she already longed for, and ... she knew it this morning with the cold certainty of treachery realised ... she had been drugged. There was

146

no other way Juan could have overridden her will. Tempted as she might have been, in her right mind she would never have succumbed.

She was angry now, angry with herself and with him. She had to root out this obsession, regain command of herself and of her life. Only a fool would remain dependent upon a relationship where there were no rewards, no love, no development or emotional, fulfilment. Of course Juan had no objection to a warm, female body, when he had need of it; but he wanted no emotional involvements and on both occasions when they'd made love, she knew her response had betrayed her, warning him that he was risking the very complication he wished to avoid. It was mortifying to Josslyn to know that the most beautiful moments in her life had meant only that to him ... a complication.

Well, she would confront him, spit out her condemnation and hatred at him, tell him how she despised him for the subterfuge that had been practised upon her. She would heap scorn upon him. Taunt him; ask him, had he become so uncertain of his own masculine attraction that he had to resort to drugging a woman to ensure her compliance?

As she rehearsed her impassioned speech, she dragged on shirt and denims, items of clothing which she fastened hastily as she heard the sound of approaching footsteps. Juan's? She would need every vestige of dignity she could muster to face him after last night's total abandon. She smoothed her silvery cap of hair, drawing herself up to her full height, waiting.

It was Manuela who entered, her dark eyes darting curiously over Josslyn's face and figure, as if she expected the intervening night to have wrought some change.

'You sleep late,' the mestizo girl observed. 'But then,' slyly, 'perhaps you did not rest much?'

'I slept perfectly well, thank you!' Josslyn snapped. It was true, she had ... too deeply and too well ... the combined influence of Juan's lovemaking and the drug. Had its hypnotic effect been combined with some aphrodisiac, she wondered, with a blush of remembrance staining her cheeks. For it seemed to her that last night had, in its intensity, transcended all her expectations, that Juan had been a more powerful, more exciting lover even than on that first occasion by the jungle pool. While she ... she had been wildly responsive, totally abandoned in her reception of him. Toes and fingers curled in an agony of self-disgust. Since Manuela remained, looking curiously at her, Josslyn added tersely, 'What do you want?'·

'I bring you an invitation!' The mestizo girl's voice held its usual insolence. 'The elders of the tribe wish to do the new bride honour. It is customary.'

'Bride?' Josslyn said bitterly. 'What bride? *You* surely don't believe in all that hocus pocus last night? You at least have been educated.'

'It is true that I have lived with the Señora de Grijalva for several years.' For once Manuela spoke gravely, with no undertones in her speech. 'But I am still a child of my people. According to our custom, you and Juan are now one.'

'And how do *you* feel about that?' Josslyn asked bluntly, thinking of the plans that had been afoot to marry Manuela to Juan.

Once more the mestizo girl's face assumed a bland inscrutability.

'It is not for me to say. Come, you must hurry. Even you must not keep the elders waiting.'

Even me? Josslyn wondered, but there were more important issues.

'And is the "bridegroom" invited to this ceremony too?' At least that would give her the chance she was waiting for, to tell him just what she thought of him; and he would not be able to exact retaliation in public, nor walk away, for fear of seeming discourteous to their hosts. But, as she followed Manuela from the hut, her plans were demolished.

'Juan is not in the village.'

'Then where is he?' Josslyn's voice rose in an alarm she could not conceal. Angry she might be with him, but he did represent her security. For his manner had convinced her that, a lone white woman in Laventa, she could be in some kind of danger. She didn't think he would lie about such a serious matter.

'I was not told, except that he is gone on tribal matters. But do not worry,' Manuela was scornful, 'as Itzpapalotl, you are quite safe. *His* name protects you.'

'What's with this "Itzpapalotl" nonsense?' Josslyn asked irritably, 'What does it mean?'

'Ask Juan!' They were approaching a seated group of people now and Manuela hastened her steps, as if she did not want to be questioned further.

The celebration, it seemed, was to take the form of a feast, for in the centre of the seated groups was a display of primitive pottery, holding nuts and berries and ... delicious aroma ... Josslyn found her mouth suddenly watering ... the savoury smell of freshly cooked fish, rice and mushrooms.

The select circle she was to join was composed only of Xchemax, the *curandera*, two elderly men, Doña Albina and Manuela. Manuela an elder? Josslyn wondered. Surely not; she must have been included out of deference to the older woman. Courteously, Xchemax indicated that Josslyn should sit between himself and the elderly Señora. Without any preliminary, Josslyn questioned Doña Albina.

'Where's Juan? Why isn't he here?'

The old woman chuckled.

'You can't expect to bind a man like Juan to your side. He will be there, when he has need of you again.'

Josslyn's face flamed, as much with anger as embarrassment. She was not a *thing* to be used at will. She was a person in her own right.

'I asked where he's gone! Is it too much to expect a

straight answer from anyone here?' But the reply she received was still evasive.

'Tribal business takes him to the next village for a day or two. Now, eat. No one else can eat until the guest of honour does so.'

Reluctantly, Josslyn stretched out her hand and helped herself to an assortment of the food. It was suprisingly palatable. But after a while, she noticed that only she was eating the fish and rice dish. She turned questioningly to Doña Albina.

'Only Quetzalcoatl and Itzpapalotl may eat of the fish from the sacred lake.'

'I just don't get this,' Josslyn complained. 'All these fancy names. I know Quetzalcoatl is some kind of god, but . . .'

'You *will* understand, presently.' Doña Albina was soothing. 'Now, eat. Manuela has prepared the special dish with her own hands. It is not to your liking?'

'It's delicious,' Joselyn admitted and she did not resist when a second helping was offered to her.

The end of the meal, it seemed, concluded the celebrations and as, with courteous bows, the elders departed, Josslyn was left once more to her own devices. Since it was obvious she was stranded here until Juan returned, she might as well fill her time usefully, she decided philosophically. It would do no harm to add to her store of sketches. She returned to her hut for her sketch block and, propped against an outer wall, began to make a series of thumbnail impressions of the scenes about her: children at play, women at work, chickens scratching the dry soil.

She must have been working for about half an hour, when she noticed a strange phenomenon. The pencil in her hand seemed to be no longer drawing what her eyes saw, or else her eyes saw strange visions. Slowly, laboriously, her hand which felt oddly heavy was covering the paper in a repetitive design . . . of snakes and birds. Sometimes a bird's head rose from the coils of a serpent; in another sketch a serpent displayed eagles' wings. It was very odd, to say the least. Yet to Josslyn it seemed that her brain was perfectly clear, though it could not, apparently, control her hand.

But her head was not to remain unaffected for long. Her pencil rolled unheeded from a hand suddenly gone numb, a numbness which she realised had also affected her legs. Despite the tropical sunshine, she was cold. Bright colours and patterns floated before her eyes. Sunstroke? she wondered hazily. But surely she must be acclimatised by now, and she had always been careful not to over-expose herself to the sun's rays.

The irridescent lines of colour began to grow into more solid shapes, shapes that advanced towards her, retreated, advanced again, but nearer. At first she delighted in their form and colour, imagined herself representing them on canvas. But then the sensation became less agreeable. Subconsciously, she knew an uneasiness which became stronger, became actual fear. Somehow she knew that in the colourful amorphous shapes, evil lurked.

Through the kaleidoscopic mist of colour, she was still aware enough to detect the outline of human forms, albeit faceless, and her brain, unusually lucid despite its delusions, could hear and understand the mutter of a voice.

'It begins. The power is working. Carry her inside.'

Gradually the influence gathered strength, until it threatened to possess her wholly, to destroy and alter her personality. She felt that she was becoming one with this evil entity. She knew the loud gasping sounds she could hear were those of her own painful breathing, Everything was dark and she recognised blindness. Panic filled her; to be blind ... never to see the wonders of the world again ... the faces of her friends ... never to be able to represent them with her pencil and brush ...

Then she was aware of hands lifting her, carrying her,

setting her down roughly on the straw, where, last night, she had known such different sensations. Finally, her blindness lending greater sensitivity to her other faculties, she sensed the departure of all but one person. She wanted to ask who was there, but her voice would not do her bidding. Then someone began to speak, in a low, monotonous, anonymous tone.

'Why did you have to come into our lives, English woman, seeking to alter that which had been ordained? Juan de Grijalva is not for you. Like his grandfather before him, he is the living Quetzalcoatl returned to his people. He bears the sign of the plumed serpent. *You* are not the true Itzpapalotl . . . how could you be? You are not of our race. Once in so many generations the man god and the woman god are reborn, the man god bearing *His* mark. Juan is such a one. He is the living Quetzalcoatl, the saviour of his people; and you have dared to come between him and tradition . . . you have dared the anger of the gods.'

Josslyn wanted to protest at the unfairness of these accusations, to tell the unknown speaker that the marriage ceremony . . . the so-called marriage ceremony . . . had been none of her doing, that she placed no credence in it. But still her voice would not obey her.

'Because you have presumed, you must die, so that the god may have his true, predestined wife. And you will die slowly, painfully. *He* cannot save you. You have deluded his human side with your feminine wiles. It is for his people to save him and we have done so. By the time he returns, you will be no more.'

Juan a god? These people really thought that? And where *was* Juan? Josslyn's soul cried out though her voice could not. He couldn't let her die. He might not want to marry her, but he was not so uncivilised, so superstitious as these people to whose mercies he had left her. Where was the Señora? Manuela? Surely even *they* constituted some protection?

The voice continued, rising in a husky chant:

'His way is not thy way, thine not his.
It is meet you should part.
I have pointed to you the road you must take.
Each to go their own way forever . . . die . . . die . . .'

But she didn't want to go, Josslyn thought confusedly.
She didn't want to be separated from Juan, whatever he
had done. *She didn't want to die!* What had they done to
her, this primitive tribe? Had they introduced some
subtle poison into her food? That *must* be it! The
curandera had been one of those present at the feast.
The feast which had purported to be in her honour had
been the means of harming her. Who knew what evil
potions the wise woman kept in her hut, among all the
fascinations and horrors Josslyn had seen; some of
which she had been allowed to sketch. Was it even
possible she had pictured the instruments of her own
death? How ironic.

Suddenly she wanted to vomit. She rolled on to her
side, retching in violent spasms. She felt as if she were
being wrenched apart, that the two halves of her had
assumed opposite personalities, striving to destroy each
other.

At last she lay back, closing her eyes. Groans escaped
her lips and weak tears ran down her face. Her head
pounded and she wondered fretfully why, at this
moment, someone had chosen to invade the malevolent
silence of the hut with angry noise.

'Where is she? What have you done to her? My God!
I'll kill whoever is responsible for this.'

Who was being so angry. Whose were the strong
arms that lifted her and carried her out of this
nightmarish hut, noisome with the stench of her own
vomit? A roaring filled her pain-filled ears, slamming,
grinding noises; then her world dissolved about her into
bumps and lurches, a mad, swaying world, where the
only stability was a softness on which her head rested,
the only comfort cool hands that soothed her brow. But

soon she was unaware of all this too, as she descended once more into her own private hell.

Weird, gloomy scenes of decay, as grotesque and fanciful as paintings by Brueghel, moved continuously before her disturbed vision. She seemed to be walking slowly, oh, so slowly, through a fantasy landscape of crumbling buildings, from whose crevices scuttled and writhed loathsome, nameless creatures. She saw blood and ritual sacrifice and knew she was seeing the downfall and destruction of ancient peoples who had died long before her time. Then everything was lost in a merciful blackness.

There were voices again ... a voice she recognised as a friendly one.

'Oh Juan!' it cried pitifully, 'Oh the poor love! To be sure she looks like death. What in the world has been happening to her?'

Bridie! Josslyn thought and she tried to mouth the name, but in vain. Her mouth was dry, her lips felt cracked and swollen, her tongue twice its normal size. But her body knew with gratitude the ministrations of Bridie's hands. She was bathed, dressed in a clean nightdress, tucked into a soft bed. But even these comforts could not dispel her private nightmares.

'I'll sit up with her,' she heard Bridie say, heard Juan's swift disclaimer.

'No, you've done enough. You need your rest now. We shall need all our strength to see her through this. You have no conception of how it will be. I'll stay. After all I *am* partly responsible for all this.'

'But Juan!' Bridie was protesting, 'You must be tired too. You've driven more than three hundred miles today.'

'Nevertheless, *madre mía*, I shall remain with Josslyn.'

Bridie's voice lowered, changed subtly.

'What will we do about ... about her?' and somehow

Josslyn knew she was no longer the subject of their conversation.

'I don't know.' For the first time Juan's strong voice faltered, betraying his weariness, a bewildered unhappiness. 'I just don't know; and for the time being there is nothing I *can* do. My place is here with Josslyn.'

And he *was* there, all the time. She knew it and took some comfort from the knowledge, as the evil within her gathered strength again. The struggle was long and fierce, a struggle from which she escaped only on the occasions when sheer exhaustion took its toll and she fell into a restless, uneasy sleep.

Throughout the worst times, it was Juan's voice she heard talking to her, comforting, reassuring, saying things that she knew must be part of her dreams.

'Fight it, Josslyn, fight it. You must! I won't *let* you die. You must come back to me. I need you. I love you.'

Sometimes, in her delirium, she laughed aloud, without any idea of why she was laughing. She talked continuously, not knowing that her words were unintelligible to her listener. Sometimes she dreamed of a blue, bird-filled paradise; sometimes the evil was there again. Often there were low, urgent voices, but somehow she knew these were real ... Bridie's, Juan's and someone whom she surmised to be a doctor. For in his presence a glass was held to her lips, she drank and for a while felt marginally better. But not for long. Another time, she woke to see a man in black soutane and white surplice standing over her, heard her own voice responding to something he had said, but what it was either of them said she could not tell. A priest, she thought. He must be. Then she must be very ill indeed. On the point of death? Bridie, being a good Catholic, would have summoned him to administer the last sacraments. Did it count, since she, Josslyn, was not of his faith? But her brain was too tired to worry. She felt resigned now, ready for death, too weak to resist.

Her illness now seemed to move into a different

phase, where she felt a searing rage against everything and everybody. She heard herself shouting words she could scarcely believe she knew; she was beating with clenched fists at someone, someone who did not fight back, but restrained her gently, tenderly.

Then, one day? One morning? One afternoon? . . . she had no idea of time's passage . . . she woke, really woke, to a great sense of weakness, but also of calm. It was as if she had returned from a long journey. Bridie was sitting at her bedside, her blue eyes full of concern the first thing Josslyn's questioning gaze encountered.

'Bridie?' she croaked, and at once the older woman rose, moved to the bedside and laid a hand upon Josslyn's brow.

'Praise be, the fever's broken. You're yourself again.'

'Have I been ill?' Josslyn asked wonderingly. She seemed to remember that she had been.

'Very ill . . .' Bridie's voice broke, 'and us thinking every breath would be your last. Sometimes I thought Juan would go out of his mind with the worry of it.'

'Juan?' Josslyn found that, with a great effort, she was able to turn her head.

'He's not here, alanna. He . . . he was called away; but he wouldn't go until he was sure you had passed the crisis.'

'What was wrong with me then?' Josslyn asked. 'Did I pick up some bug in the swampland?'

'You don't remember?' Bridie asked curiously and, as the girl shook her head, 'Then it's best we leave explanations until you're stronger. Do you think you could drink a little warm milk, or some soup?'

Little by little, day by day, Josslyn regained her strength, until the time came, when, leaning on Bridie's arm, she could walk slowly and painfully out on to the patio, to lie gratefully in a reclining chair, her face turned up to the sun.

Bridie drew up a chair beside her and it seemed a good moment to question her about recent events of which, until now, she'd had only the dimmest memories. But certain facts had returned to trouble her.

'What *was* wrong with me, Bridie?' She thought the other woman hesitated before she replied.

'Food poisoning of . . . of some kind.'

'Food poisoning! Was anyone else affected?'

'No.'

There was something so flat, so uncommunicative in Bridie's reply that Josslyn realised intuitively that there was more underlying the statement. It seemed incredible and yet . . .

'Bridie? Did someone deliberately poison me?'

Bridget de Grijalva stared at her young guest with something like despair in the blue eyes so like her son's. Then, slowly, she nodded.

'But who? Who would do a thing like that? Why?'

'Juan made me promise not to discuss it, until he could be here. He . . . he wants to explain it to you himself. He said . . . he said there had been enough misunderstandings between you.'

'Well for once he spoke the truth!' Josslyn said bitterly. So far as Juan was concerned, she had total recall. 'How much did he tell you of what went on at Laventa?'

'Everything!' Bridie said in a low tone. 'He . . . we thought you were dying. He sat with you night and day, until the doctor made him rest. I sat with him some of the time, and it all came out, as though he just had to unburden himself.'

'It must have been quite a shock for you,' Josslyn said grimly, 'to discover just how despicable your own son is.'

'Despicable?' Bridie looked and sounded surprised. 'Oh no, my dear! I think he's acted very sensibly throughout, in view of . . . well . . . what he knew. I only wish he'd confided in me before. But he's always been one to bear his own burdens. And now he's acted honourably.'

Josslyn's eyebrows shot up.

'Honourably? Sensibly? Are we talking about the same man, the same story? Or has he filled you up with a load of lies?'

'Josslyn!' Bridie chided. 'You're talking about my son, and I'm afraid I can't listen if . . . if you're going to denigrate him.' She rose with dignity and made her way to the door. 'If you have any differences to settle with him . . .' Remembering that Josslyn had been so ill, her face and voice softened a little, 'and there are always differences at the beginning of a relationship . . . then you must sort them out with Juan, when he comes home.'

'I shan't be here then, not if I can help it,' Josslyn retorted, but her protest was wasted; Bridie had already left the room, softly closing the door behind her.

Alone, Josslyn pondered on Bridie's final words, 'the beginning of a relationship'. If Juan had told his mother everything, that implied that he had told her about the primitive 'marriage ceremony'; but surely Bridie would place no more consequence upon that than Josslyn herself did, unless he had also told his mother about his promise that a civil ceremony should be performed when they returned to Mexico City? But then Josslyn was positive he hadn't meant a word of that. It had just been a sop to her conscience . . . to lull her into a false sense of security . . . to ensure her willing response to his lovemaking.

But suppose now, assuming that he felt the guilt Bridie claimed, felt that the attempt oin her life was *his* fault, suppose he now intended to make that civil ceremony an actuality once he returned . . . once Josslyn was fit enough? Would she want to be married to him under those circumstances? At first she thought she would be willing to do so under *any* circumstances, so long as she might spend the rest of her life with him. But then common sense prevailed. A marriage founded on such a basis could not work. She couldn't settle for anything less than genuine, whole-hearted love and that she could never have from Juan. The words of love she'd believed him to have spoken had just been part of her hallucinatory dreams.

Her determination to be gone before Juan returned was reinforced. She would not stay to be an object of his guilt, his charity. From that moment, Josslyn worked towards regaining her strength with the determination she gave to every undertaking.

'Well, I can't stop you. But I'm surprised . . . yes, and *hurt*!'

Josslyn paused in her packing.

'Oh Bridie, please don't make it worse; please don't be offended. I've no wish to upset *you*, or to seem ungrateful for all you've done for me. But I just *can't* be here when Juan comes home. He can't have told you everything or you'd understand that.'

'And you'll not even give the lad a chance to defend himself?'

'No.' She dared not. His tongue was too glib and this, taken in conjunction with those other attributes of his . . . his compelling masculinity, the domination his body had already attained over hers . . . would, she feared, too easily overcome her resolution. 'My mind's made up and my flight home is arranged. And besides, I have a book to write.' Determinedly, she thrust more items into her suitcase.

'A book you wouldn't be able to write, but for him,' Bridie pointed out.

'Oh, I don't know. The drawing will be mine, the text mine. Any guide would have done just as well. In fact I didn't really need a guide. I didn't need him to get me to Laventa. I managed to get *there* without him.'

'Maybe. But you nearly didn't come back! Josslyn, I've never told you this because I thought you'd be here, that Juan would be able to tell you himself. The portraits you painted, before you left for Laventa . . .'

Josslyn had almost forgotten them. They seemed to have been executed in another time, another world. Only the memory of her time with the Olmecs, which was slowly returning to her, seemed to have any reality; and now that these memories had lost their terror, she longed to write of them, to picture them. If only she could capture on canvas the nightmarish conjurings of the hallucinatory drugs.

'What about the portraits?' she asked almost disinterestedly. Her packing was finished, her taxi due at any moment.

'Juan saw them. He . . .'

'Oh? Did he like them?' Josslyn was only mildly curious. She really didn't care any more.

'He recognised your expertise,' Bridie said carefully, 'but he wasn't looking at them as works of art, but for what they revealed . . . the characters of the sitters.'

Josslyn was momentarily gratified. So she hadn't lost her skill.

'He thought I'd captured something of their personalities?'

Somewhere below, a hooter sounded its strident summons and Josslyn swung her case off the bed.

'Yes, you captured them very well indeed . . . fortunately for you.'

Josslyn bent and kissed Bridie's soft cheek.

'Don't think too badly of me, Bridie. I'll always remember you with affection and gratitude. You've been very good to me.'

Bridie followed her out of the room and along the landing, down the stairs.

'Don't you want to know what Juan saw in your paintings?'

Running lightly down the front steps, Josslyn called back over her shoulder.

'I *know* what he saw . . . what I saw myself: a remarkable old lady, incredibly beautiful for her age; and a *young* beautiful woman.' She opened the rear door of the taxi, thrusting her suitcase in before her. 'The airport please ... *pronto!*'

'He saw evil in the eyes ... evil towards you.' Bridie called after her. 'That's what brought him to Laventa in such a hurry.' But her words were lost as Josslyn slammed the door, waving as the taxi shot away from a standing start, catapulting her back in her seat.

Regaining her equilibrium with some difficulty, Josslyn felt herself relax at last. She'd done it. She'd made it. She'd escaped from the villa before Juan returned. It might be taking the coward's way out, but at least she hadn't to face him with the awareness of all that lay between them, or hear any arguments he might add to his mother's about her departure. In actual fact, her precipitate flight was probably quite unnecessary. Josslyn thought it very unlikely that he would be troubled by her absence. He would probably be only too glad to be rid of her and the complication she represented, the complication of her having fallen in love with him, despite all his warnings.

But it was better for her peace of mind, wasn't it, that she shouldn't see him again, however much her heart and body ached to do so?

Daphne Ransome and Harry Livings accorded Josslyn a warm welcome home, tinged with relief on Daphne's part, curiosity on Harry's. He was anxious to see if Josslyn could produce work comparable with that of her late father.

'Darling, you look so thin and drawn!' Daphne exclaimed. 'Have you been ill, and not told me, you naughty girl?'

Josslyn could imagine Daphne's reactions if she were to learn how close her daughter had come to death, and she brushed the comment aside.

'Just the heat, and a slight fever ... nothing to worry about.'

She was as evasive about the material she had brought

back, refusing to allow anyone to see photographs or preliminary drawings.

'When they're fit to be seen,' she insisted to parent and publisher alike.

Then she shut herself away, as Daphne complained, for weeks on end, emerging only for meals, meals which she rarely finished, so that she became even more pale and fine drawn. Josslyn was determined, though more recent visual experiences filled her mind, to execute her work in chronological order and she made a start, therefore, with the scenes from Eliseo's village. Even here though, she could not escape the tentacles of primitive superstition as she portrayed the ceremony she'd witnessed in the disused church. The snake! She shuddered. There was no escaping the fact that its influence would permeate her book.

After much heart-searching, reluctantly she included the sketch of Juan mastering the steer, having convinced herself that it would be unprofessional of her to leave out such an important aspect of the villagers' life for her own personal motives.

Some of the sketches were less evocative of emotion in their content: artifacts, fragments of carved masonry, simple domestic scenes. But, inevitably, she reached the point where she must detail the experiences gained at Laventa. Here, too, she began with the less traumatic moments ... children at play, the women at their weaving. But then came the flesh creeping contents of the *curandera*'s hut, with its reminder that here, perhaps, lay the clue to her sickness, her near death.

She could not omit the scenes of the 'marriage ceremony', but self-preservation made her depict the principals as an Olmec man and woman. Her nightmarish illusions she might be prepared to share with an avid reading public, but not something which affected her so intimately, something which still had the power to send dagger-like shafts of pain through her, as she forced herself to accept the fact that she would never see Juan de Grijalva again, much less know the ecstasy of his possession, of her own response, the joy of mutual giving.

Finally, climatically, though she wished she might omit them, there returned to her graphic memories of her hallucinatory experiences, the last two or three illustrations in her book containing all the horror, the glimpses of the hell into which she had descended.

The book called for little in the way of text ... mere explanatory notes in most cases; but it was almost a therapeutic exercise to end in a slightly more detailed vein with a relation of her extraordinary illness ... though she forebore to mention that it had been induced by deliberate ill will on the part of a person or persons unknown.

But at last the task was finished and she emerged from her study feeling that she had exorcised at least some of the ghosts. Amerindian superstition and sorcery could not touch her, here in the blessed sanity of home. What she could not escape from, at first, were the haunting memories of Juan and her misguided love for him.

Harry Livings was curious, startled by her flat insistence that nowhere in her book should any mention be made of Juan de Grijalva.

'I wish you'd never sent me to him,' she insisted. 'I could well have done without his help.' And without the unhappiness his acquaintance brought, she added inwardly.

'Surely the chap's at least entitled to a mention in the credits? And what about the people who allowed you into their lives, their homes? In your early letters home, you were full of ideas about allocating some of your royalties to helping them achieve decent living standards. You seemed quite impressed by de Grijalva's own work for his countrymen.'

That had been before she had recognised his self-interest ... that it lay in playing on the superstitious beliefs of his distant relations, distant from him in blood and in culture.

'Well I've changed my mind. I'm entitled to do that? It *is* my book!'

She remained adamant; and as the months went by, between the completion of her work and the arrival of the final proofs, she endeavoured to thrust all thoughts of Juan from her mind; and when that was totally impossible, she deliberately lashed herself into a fury over the wrongs he had done her, until, finally, by publication date, she believed herself cured, believed that she could remake her life, live contentedly without Juan, who, she had convinced herself by now, was the most despicable man on God's earth.

Then had come the day of the publishers' party, the launch of *Mexican Sketchbook*.

CHAPTER EIGHT

JUAN slept on peacefully in the middle of Josslyn's bed. In sleep, the firm lines of his mouth softened, as though he smiled. Tired as she was, cramped from sitting so long in the chair, she just couldn't bring herself to occupy the remaining space. She could still remember all too vividly lying even closer to him than that would entail . . . And if he should wake, find her unguarded in sleep?

How she had wished, many times since, that she hadn't put all her efforts into persuading him to rescind his refusal to take her into the interior. If his refusal had held good, she might have been furious at the time, but how much heartache and danger it might have saved her. Yet, like a fool, she had promised to follow his advice implicitly. It hadn't been a surrender of her independence, she'd assured herself at the time, just expediency . . . a necessary compromise to ensure the success of her visit to Mexico, the continuance of the tradition her father had begun; and, though she hadn't admitted it to herself at the time, there had been her reluctance for their acquaintance to be cut short so peremptorily.

The bedside telephone rang, startling in the silence, interrupting her musings, and immediately Josslyn's hand went to the receiver, hoping to quell the noise before it disturbed Juan. He was safer asleep. But she was not quick enough. Those familiar, lightning reactions of his made him swifter than her. At once he was wide awake, the instrument in his hand.

'Yes? Room 270? I don't know. Just a minute. Josslyn, *is* this Room 270?'

'Yes, who wants to know?' She held out her hand for

the receiver, but he kept it out of her reach. 'It must be for me,' she hissed.

'This is Juan de Grijalva speaking.' He ignored Josslyn's frantic attempts to gain possession of the telephone. 'Who is that, please?' A pause, then, 'Ah, Mrs Ransome, of course. We've met, but only briefly, I didn't recognise your voice.'

'My mother?' Josslyn could feel the blood draining from her face. Whatever must her mother be thinking? She glanced at her watch. Three a.m.! Had she really sat here so long, completely lost in reminiscence? 'Kindly allow me to take my own telephone calls,' she snapped.

'Certainly.' To her surprise, he made no demur. But he made her sit on the side of the bed to take the call and one of his arms held her there, his head resting against her, so that she could feel the soft silk of his beard brushing the swell of her breast, so that when she spoke to Daphne, her voice was slightly breathless.

'Mother?'

'Yes, of course! Joss, darling, what *is* that man doing in your room . . . and at this time of night?'

Josslyn felt a little light-headed. It must be fatigue . . . or the sensual urges she was experiencing, for Juan's hand was now curved around her body, just above the waistline, his fingers cupping her breast, the soft material of the Grecian dress no protection against the insidious warmth of his flesh.

'What difference does the time of day make?' she asked a trifle hysterically. 'Would it make it any more respectable if it was daylight?'

'Joss!' Daphne demanded sharply, 'Are you drunk?'

She was, but not with alcohol. She was drunk with sensations she thought she'd forgotten . . . or at least had not permitted herself to think about these last six months.

'No, Mother!' She tried to speak more rationally. 'No, I'm not drunk. I just . . . I wasn't expecting you to phone me in the middle of the night.'

'Evidently!' Daphne said drily. 'I rang because Harry and I have something to tell you . . . but I think perhaps it had better wait. Joss, you're too old for me to tell you what you should or shouldn't be doing, but I won't pretend I'm not surprised and . . . yes . . . shocked.'

'Mother, please. You don't understand . . .'

'Oh, I think I do, Joss. I can remember what it's like to be young and in love, but I would have preferred it if . . .'

'But I'm not in love, Mother, I'm *not*!' It was a desperate attempt to convince herself . . . *and* the man who listened. But she had been in love once, when the jungle had become for her a paradise, far away from the inhibiting mores of civilisation, when it had seemed so right, so in keeping with their idyllic surroundings.

'But Josslyn, if you're not in love with him,' Daphne Ransome worried, 'why is he in your room? Joss, everything *is* all right isn't it? I mean, you didn't seem very pleased to see Señor de Grijalva, and you have been . . . well . . . rather quiet since you came home. He . . . he isn't threatening you in any way? You wouldn't like me to call the police, or . . . or send Harry up?'

'No! Good heavens! It's nothing like that, Mother. I can explain, but . . . but it's a bit awkward just now.'

'Very!' a voice loudly in her ear . . . loudly enough for Mrs Ransome to overhear. Peremptorily, the receiver was removed from Josslyn's hand and Juan spoke once more into the mouthpiece. 'Mrs Ransome, perhaps we could all discuss this in the morning? Perhaps I should say *later* this morning? Josslyn and I have a lot to straighten out before then.'

'We certainly do!' Josslyn hissed furiously, but he ignored her. He was still listening politely, his face expressionless and, helplessly, Josslyn tried to imagine what her mother could be saying to him. Then, with a courteous, 'Of course. Good night, Mrs Ransome,' he returned the receiver to its rest and turned his attention to Josslyn.

'Now,' he said throatily. His hold upon her tightened and, despite her resistance, he pulled her down to lie beside him, dark blue eyes interestedly surveying the valley between her breasts, now revealed to him. His hand moved to caress, to possess.

She had told her mother that Juan posed no threat to her. Nor did he ... not in the terms of violence Daphne had feared ... but he *did* pose a threat in another way: to her only recently regained peace of mind; to her resolution, one which frankly she had never expected to have put to the test. She had not expected that she would ever see Juan de Grijalva again. She couldn't think why he had bothered to come here. It wasn't as if the situation between them would ever be any different.

'I was trying to explain to my mother,' she told him icily, as she tried to push away the offending hand, 'that she had no cause for concern that ... that ...'

'That my presence in your bedroom, in the small hours of the morning, was totally innocent? And do you think she believed you ... when you don't believe it yourself?'

'Of course she didn't believe me!' Josslyn was furious. 'Oh how *dare* you put me in ... in this position?'

'Position? *This* one?' he asked, laughter in his voice, as he clamped the whole length of her to his lean, muscular body. As he attempted further intimacies, she fought him, tooth and claw.

'What makes you think that you can just walk back into my life and behave like this? After ... after everything ... the abominable way you treated me ... the underhand ... lying ...'

'Be still!' he growled, restraining her with ease. 'Anyone would think we were complete strangers. But it isn't so, is it? Mmm!' He murmured against her breasts. 'I *like* you in this dress. But I'd like you better without it. Our bodies know each other, even if our souls do not. Relax, *querida*,' he whispered, as she renewed her attempts to escape. 'You know you want this as much as I do. You've always wanted it, right from the first.'

Not *right* from the first, Josslyn thought hazily. Oh, the physical attraction had been there; that was true enough. But she hadn't wanted to be attracted to Juan in that way. She'd fought the sensation at first, telling herself that it was impossible she should feel that way about a man she hardly knew, whom she was sure she disliked, of whose principles she could not approve, reminding herself that it would be sheer lunacy to become involved with a man who put his freedom before all other considerations, who believed in the gratification of his baser instincts, but had nothing to offer on a mental or spiritual plane.

'And since we're married, there's no reason . . .'

'Married!' Josslyn almost shrieked the word at him. 'I don't know how you have the brazen effrontery to refer to that . . . that primitive ritual. I don't know a lot about Catholics, but I *do* know that they take marriage pretty seriously . . . and to drug me, so that I didn't know what I was doing, just so that you could . . . could . . . I won't even dignify it by the words "make love". It was just animal lust, aroused by that disgusting dancing of theirs . . .'

'Hold on, hold on!' Juan sat up straight, glaring down at her. 'What do you mean, drugged? I did nothing of the sort. We made love that night in way I haven't been able to forget since; that I want to repeat, over and over again. You didn't make any protests then . . . you were willing, ardent . . .'

'Because I didn't know what I was doing. I was drugged I tell you,' and, as he continued to look genuinely incredulous, 'OK. So maybe *you* didn't know anything about it; maybe it was the same person who tried to poison me. They seem to know a lot about that sort of thing, your Olmecs.'

But Juan was shaking his head.

'No. It wouldn't have been the same person. If an

aphrodisiac was given to you, it would have been by
someone who desired the consummation of our . . .'

'Don't you dare say "marriage" again.'

'But we *are* married. No, hear me out. I thought you'd
be willing to anticipate any formal ceremony. After all,'
he said drily, 'we had made love before. Of course I don't
believe in the validity of the ceremony performed at
Laventa, any more than you do, but I didn't want to
offend Xchemax. He was eager for it to take place!'

'Why should *he* want us to be married?' Josslyn was
momentarily diverted.

'Because he wanted Manuela for himself. He wanted
me out of the running where she was concerned. Not
that I was even *in* the running . . .'

'Manuela? But surely *she* had something to say
about that?'

'She said "yes",' Juan said simply. 'She'd been in love
with Xchemax since she was a child. Then my
grandmother brought her to Mexico City, filled her
head with a lot of nonsense about being the chosen one
. . . as *she* had been . . . and she genuinely enjoyed what
civilisation could give her. But underneath that veneer,
she remained, though she might not have realised it
herself, very much a child of Laventa; and when you
took her back there and she met Xchemax again, she
knew where her true destiny lay.'

Josslyn spared a moment to wonder over the strange
nature of love . . . that a girl who had become
accustomed to luxury could willingly go back to a
primitive existence. But wasn't *she* the same? If only
she could have the assurance of Juan's love, she knew
she would follow him anywhere . . . well, almost
anywhere. If *he* wanted to go and live with his Olmecs,
that might be too dangerous for her. Someone at
Laventa hated her . . . wanted her dead. But then she
remembered and returned to the attack.

'Then if you don't believe in the ceremony, how can
you claim we're married?'

'Because we are,' he persisted. 'Is it possible that you genuinely don't remember?' Thoughtfully, 'I suppose it is. We never knew when you were lucid or hallucinating. Do you really not remember the priest coming to your bedside at the villa? You seemed to give your promise willingly enough, and I thought . . .'

Josslyn's brow wrinkled in thought.

'I do remember the priest . . . I think,' she said slowly. 'But I thought he was there because I was going to die. I certainly felt as if I was going to. *They* told me I would die.'

'They?'

'The voices . . . in the hut. It was so dark; I think whatever they'd given me had made me blind too. But I could hear them, even though I couldn't see or speak. But nothing of what they said made sense . . . except that I must die for presuming to marry you.'

'Yes,' he said wearily. 'I know about that and I understand. But you may find it hard to do so . . . to accept. It sounds crazy, unless you first know the people, their history, their religion. I told you the Indians only partially accepted Christianity, the parts that suited them; that to them Christ was a reincarnation of their own god. Throughout the centuries they and their descendants looked for his return. Even after their betrayal by Cortes, the Indians still went on waiting for their saviour, Quetzalcoatl. His name, by the way, was made up of two words: "Quetzal", a bird that lives up in the mists of the tropical mountains, a bird symbolising heaven and spiritual energy; and "coatl", the serpent, denoting earth and material forces. So his symbolic and religious observances became that of the plumed serpent, *la serpiente plumosa*.' He thrust out his forearm for her inspection. 'See that?'

'Yes, I noticed it a long time ago . . . and I think I'm ahead of you; I think I realised it way back. The Indians see that as a sign, don't they? They think *you're* their serpent god?' And did he believe himself to be divine? If he did it was presumption, arrogance ... blasphemy, surely, according to the dictates of his religion? Juan came of a Catholic family. Did Bridie know about this? she wondered. She asked.

'Yes, but she couldn't understand, any more than you apparently do. My father, fortunately for him, escaped being born with the mark. Olmec tradition has always foretold the return of their god as a white man, a fair god who would come to them, teach them to farm, to read and write, to improve their lot.'

'It's quite ridiculous!'

'Ridiculous? To western eyes maybe ...'

'But, Juan, it's wrong, too! Setting yourself up as a god. What about "thou shalt not have strange gods before me?" You're committing the sin of pride ... of blasphemy ...'

'Josslyn! Josslyn! *I've* never claimed to be anything more than I am, an ordinary man with a fervent desire to help my underprivileged countrymen. I don't just work among the Olmec. I try to help *all* isolated tribes. I thought you realised that. Remember Eliseo's village? No, the claim is all on the side of the Olmecs.'

She pulled away from him and sat on the side of the bed, her golden eyes accusing.

'Then you should deny it! Explain!'

He sighed in exasperation, stood up and began to pace the room, his hands clasping and unclasping as he sought to make her understand.

'They just wouldn't believe me. Their tradition is too strong. Their parents believed that my grandfather was a god. Yes, he bore the sign. My grandmother believed it. He came to their village quite by accident ... an explorer, sick with some tropical disease he'd picked up in their swampland. He came out of the swamp at the edge of the sacred lake; he was blond, bearded. My grandmother ... she was the *curandera* then ... nursed him back to health. She fell in love with him. It may

have been expediency, too, because it had been foretold
at her birth that she would marry a god ... give birth to
gods ... be the salvation of her race. But I think she
genuinely loved him. And he, God help him, fell in love
with her, ignorant and untutored as she was. But she
was beautiful. Remember Manuela? My grandmother
must have looked just as she did as a child.'

'If you find her so attractive,' Josslyn said waspishly,
'I'm surprised you didn't go along with your
grandmother's plans and marry the girl.'

He moved rapidly, stood over her, his hands
compellingly on her shoulders.

'Josslyn! I never intended, or wanted, to marry
Manuela. I never intended to marry anyone ... not in
my grandmother's lifetime at least.'

'Your *grandmother* really believes in all this nonsense?
But she's ...'

'An Indian at heart, with only the veneer of
civilisation ... perhaps a slightly thicker veneer than
Manuela managed to achieve. I was born,' he continued
soberly, 'only hours after my grandfather died ... and I
bore the sign, the birthmark, so she believed his spirit
had passed into me. But I'm *not* like my grandfather,
Josslyn, you must believe that. I look like him, but he
was proud and arrogant and, I think, a little insane.
Perhaps he never quite recovered from that illness. He
really came to believe that he was a god. He revelled in
it. I don't know this of my own experience, you
understand, only from what my father told me.'

'So then the only person who would resent your
marrying me ...' she stared at him with dawning,
horrified realisation in her eyes, 'would be ...'

'*Mía abuelita,*' he agreed wearily. 'I think, when she
reached her native village once more, all the inhibitions
produced by civilisation fell away from her. Unwisely,
Xchemax revealed to her his feelings for Manuela. She
knew she hadn't much longer to live and she wanted to
see Manuela and I married, carrying on, as she

supposed, the traditions she and my grandfather had upheld. Even though my grandfather had the villa in Mexico City, they spent long periods of time at Laventa, until he became too frail to make the journey. Then my grandmother remained, watching me grow up, waiting "for my time to come", as she put it.'

'But she didn't succeed in influencing you?' she asked disbelievingly.

'Not in the way you mean. Fortunately,' his tone was dry, 'my parents insisted on a European education for me. My father was a very down-to-earth man, a great disappointment to my grandmother. He detested what my grandfather had become. That's why he spent very little time at home; and he married a shrewd, practical Irishwoman! But because I wanted to help the Amerindian tribes, to better their lifestyle without destroying their culture, my grandmother believed she had prevailed.'

'And *your grandmother* tried to poison me? Damn it! She succeeded! What did she use?'

'Psilocybin mushrooms. They've always been used by the Indian tribes in religious and social rituals. That's why the Olmecs have always been considered to be magicians, because they've learned to use drugs, gained from mushroom and cactus plants, to cause a state of hallucination ... that is, in small doses. Taken in overdose they can produce convulsions and finally death. Thank God I managed to escape her agents.'

'Escape? Her agents?'

'Yes,' he said grimly. 'Two fellows ... slaves ... whom she ordered to do her will. They got me to a nearby settlement on the pretence of medical help being needed there. The place was uninhabited, and they tied me up and left me in one of the deserted huts.'

'Two slaves dared to lay hands on the serpent god?' Josslyn said incredulously.

'Two slaves not of the Olmec race,' he reminded her. 'To them I was just an unimportant European man.'

'So how *did* you escape?'

'Xchemax and Manuela had their suspicions about my disappearance. I should have been at that feast. They both knew my grandmother's wishes about my marriage, and when she was so complaisant about us it didn't ring true. And of course Xchemax knew the neighbouring village was deserted. So when the so-called celebration was over, Manuela drove to the settlement, found me and released me . . .'

'But it was Manuela who prepared the fish and mushrooms . . .'

'She thought they were ordinary mushrooms. She didn't know of the substitution, but she found the fact that I'd been called away on a wild goose chase suspicious. Without Manuela I might not have reached you in time, got you back to Mexico City and medical treatment. Manuela agreed to help me . . . looked after you, while I drove like a maniac.'

'And I thought at first it was Manuela who hated me . . .'

'I think she did resent you at first. Perhaps if she had never gone with you to Laventa . . .' he shrugged. 'I was against her leaving her native village in the first place. The Indians need better conditions, but too much of their history has already disappeared. If they leave their villages . . .'

'And you don't feel an urge to convert them to Christianity?'

Juan shook his head.

'My concern is with their physical well-being. Their souls I leave to the priests.'

Josslyn wanted to believe him, believe that he was no egocentric, like his grandfather.

'But if you had no part in their worship of you, why did you call your shop Quetzalcoatl?' she challenged.

Juan laughed.

'By pure coincidence it was named that when I

bought the premises and it appealed to my somewhat warped sense of humour to keep it so.'

Doubts still lurked.

'You *did* encourage Manuela originally, though? You told me once that she'd shared your tent . . .' She broke off as he threw back his blond head in amused laughter.

'I *knew* you'd taken that the wrong way. My exact words were that both Manuela and my mother had shared my tent. They did! Together!'

'*Why* did you marry me?' Josslyn probed. 'To ease your conscience, in case I died? Yes . . .' she said slowly, 'you thought I was going to die; you thought you wouldn't be inconvenienced by having a wife for very long.'

'Josslyn!' he protested. He came to sit beside her, but she edged away.

'But you miscalculated. I didn't die . . .'

'Thank God. Damn it, Josslyn!' He seized her by the upper arms. 'Just what kind of a monster do you think I am? Will you just shut up for a moment and listen.'

'No!' Her golden eyes glared at him. 'I think I've listened to you for long enough. You've explained your involvement with the Olmecs. OK. So now I know what was wrong with me and who was responsible. I don't want to hear any more.'

'What you want, right at this moment,' he ground out the words, 'is immaterial. You're *going* to hear me out . . . right to the end; and if after that you're still as disbelieving, as stubborn . . .'

'Yes?' she challenged him.

'Then you can go to hell by your own route . . . and it *will* be hell, Josslyn, because whatever you try to tell me to the contrary, however much you deny it,' his voice became rife with sensuality, 'I *know* you want me, need me, as much as I want you.' The lancing blue eyes, steady as steel, dared her to speak the words of denial that trembled on her lips and, never one to be willingly subjugated, she parted them, made the attempt. But the words were not destined to be uttered ... were stillborn against the firm, compelling pressure of his mouth, the breath crushed from her body by the hard proximity of his.

'You're only half alive without me ... I'm incomplete without you,' he muttered as his lips trailed fire down the slender column of her throat. 'Admit it! Tell me what these last few months have been like.'

They had been like a never-ending famine, a soul-parching drought, but she was not going to admit it to *him*.

'It is possible for a woman to be a valid person without having a man around all the time,' she countered. 'Women have other needs besides those of a sexual relationship.'

'Of course,' he retorted fiercely, 'but you were also made for love ... for passion. Think back, Josslyn! Remember the times we made love! Can you deny the sensations you felt then? Don't you remember telling me that you loved me?'

An incredible anger shook her, because she could *not* deny it, but also because he should so callously remind her of what she'd sought to forget ... the impetuous words that had so shamefully betrayed her. She strained away from him.

'People will say anything in the heat of a moment like that ... even men ... And besides,' she added bitterly, 'what was your reaction? Do *you* remember *that*? You threw my words back in my face, said there would never be another time. You even accused me of trying to trap you, of making you take my virginity. Have you conveniently forgotten that? And yet,' she accused, 'you still couldn't leave me alone. You wouldn't let me find another guide, you followed me to Laventa ...'

'I *had* to!' he exploded, 'Knowing what I knew, seeing what I saw in those painted eyes ...'

'Whose?'

'My grandmother's, of course. I thought you claimed to be so perceptive, to be able to portray character . . .'

'I am . . . I do. But I can't always tell what the expression *means*. But I suppose *you're* so clever . . .'

'It wasn't cleverness,' he interrupted impatiently, 'just an insight, born of long acquaintance with *la abuelita*. I knew her plans for me, knew what she was capable of if I went against her. Why do you think I refused to entertain the idea of marriage during her lifetime? Why I let her think I was seriously considering marrying Manuela?'

'That was your only reason?'

'No,' he admitted, 'but it was a very strong one. Josslyn, I was unwise enough to let my grandmother see how I felt towards you. It was only a momentary lapse, yet she was quick-witted enough to perceive it. But when I went away, I thought you'd be safe enough in my mother's part of the house. I never dreamt you would go off into the jungle, or that my grandmother would accompany you.'

'Juan? Just what *did* you see in that portrait?'

'Something fearful, primitive,' he said slowly, soberly, his handsome features becoming haggard at the memory, 'a terrible, ancient hatred; the kind of hatred that once made Indian destroy Indian in tribal warfare . . . a fanaticism born of long-held religious beliefs. I *knew* your life was in danger.'

'So instead of taking me away from Laventa,' Josslyn's tone was sarcastic, 'you went through a form of marriage with me, calculated to annoy her even further.'

'I thought . . .' Juan sounded inexpressibly weary again. 'I thought that, if I married you according to Olmec tradition, gave you, in the Indian's sight, the protection of Quetzalcoatl's name . . . made you Itzpapalotl, his traditional bride, that my grandmother's superstitious awe of the gods would protect you.'

'Well it didn't,' she pointed out unnecessarily.

'No. I miscalculated the strength of her will, her belief that, as my ancestress, herself regarded as a goddess, she could command me.' His mood changed, became urgent. 'Josslyn, we've talked enough. We've already wasted half a year apart. Let's not waste any more time.' He tried to draw her back into his arms, but Josslyn evaded him. She could not shake off her doubts so easily.

'Six months! Yes, it took you six months to come and find me ... to tell me all this. Did it take you that long to work out a good story?' She expected retaliation, anger, not the look of resignation, of sorrow.

'It took six months for my grandmother to die ... What would you have had me do, Josslyn? Drag her back to Mexico City? Hand her over to the authorities for attempted murder? Whatever she'd done, she was still my grandmother and I still had a very great affection for her ... she for me. Perhaps you think I shouldn't have forgiven her, stayed with her to prove that forgiveness?'

'No ... no, of course not ... I'm sorry ...' she managed to say, though she did not think *she* would ever be able to forgive Doña Albina's attempt on her life. 'You ... you said you had *other* reasons for staying single,' she reminded him, anxious suddenly to drive the look of sadness from his face.

A great breath of exasperation escaped him and he flung himself backwards on the bed, hands clasped behind his head; and now, contrarily, Josslyn longed to lean over him, to press herself to the hardness of his body, seduce him with loving words and kisses. But her rejection had been too effective. He was serious now, passion forgotten, concentrating on her query.

'I told you once what sort of man I am ... that I need to travel.' He smiled wryly. 'I suppose it's in my blood, however much I deplore my heritage. And in my experience, once a woman forms an emotional attachment, she becomes clinging, tries to curtail a man's freedom. I've always been a free agent; expected to remain so.'

'So what's different?' Josslyn said, unable to prevent the pique that evidenced itself in her voice. He must be regretting the legalisation of their marriage. 'I'm not going to hold you to a ceremony that I can't even remember. I'm not asking you to give up your freedom. Our relationship was purely a business one so far as I'm concerned.'

'*Was* being the operative word.' His eyes met hers, blue depths sleepy, languorous, making her nerves quiver. 'It didn't remain that way, did it?'

'That was *your* fault,' she snapped. 'You ... you seduced me. In spite of all your carping about "non-involvement" you just couldn't resist trying to see if I was susceptible to your ... your ...'

'You're right about my not being able to resist!' He came upright in one lithe, easy movement, bringing him too close again. 'But it was *you* I couldn't resist. At first I thought I *could* travel with you, remain immune to all that you were. Fool that I was!'

Josslyn didn't know whether to feel flattered or insulted. Flattered because he'd found her attractive, insulted because he'd castigated himself as a fool for doing so.

'I can't give up my travelling,' he said bluntly, 'particularly the travel involved in my work among the tribes. I don't have the same motives as my grandparents, but I do care greatly for their welfare. I'm fascinated by their customs, their heritage ... which is also, in part, mine.' He waxed enthusiastic, hands clasped around his knees, almost boyish in his eagerness. 'There's still so much to be discovered ... archaeological finds that need to be preserved for future generations. My work is closely linked with the Archaeological Societies of Mexico.'

'I know. Your grandmother told me about your degree, that you'd been responsible for the recovery of several valuable items ... that they were in the city museums.'

'So you *do* understand just how important all this is to me?'

'Of course!' She was surprised that he should think her incapable of such understanding. '*I* have a career that matters to *me* ... that I don't want to give up.'

'So that's why I felt I couldn't risk any emotional involvements, having to tear myself away from clinging wife every time I had to go away ... the emotionally dependant make very high demands on their partner.'

'Did it never occur to you,' Josslyn asked casually, 'to look for a wife who might be prepared to travel with you? Or who had a career of her own to keep her occupied? Someone mature enough to accept your way of life?'

Juan laughed shortly.

'In my experience such paragons are few and far between.'

'And yet, so you claim, you married *me*! Why, for heaven's sake?'

'Because, confound it ...' There was self-mockery in his tone, 'I *wanted* to marry you. I found I couldn't do without you and, in spite of what you think of me, I do have some principles. I respect you too much to offer you anything less.' His compelling eyes probed hers, attempting to invade the most secret recesses of her soul, before they travelled slowly and with deliberate sensuality, his glance in itself a physical caress. 'I want you, Josslyn. I wanted you from the first moment I saw you, though I tried to crush the feeling ... told myself it was impossible ...'

Josslyn found herself trembling, but he wasn't going to disarm her so easily.

'Your respect for me didn't seem to bother you the first time,' she said, her voice low.

'I didn't know you as well as I do now. I believed you to be experienced. You talked, behaved, like an emancipated woman.'

'Then you believe a woman is just as free as a man to be experienced?'

'No!' Then he qualified the explosive negative. 'At least, not the woman *I* take for my wife. When I discovered you were a virgin, I can't tell you how I felt. At first I hated myself, hated you for the trick I thought you'd played on me. But it was mingled with a sense of elation . . . of wonder . . . that I had been the first with you. Oh, Josslyn!' His arm curved about her shoulders, his hand seeking the curve of her breast.

'Then you've changed your mind about what you want in a wife.' She was careful not to show her disappointment. 'Because I *am* emancipated, Juan . . . even my mother accuses me of being unfeminine. I won't submit to the slave syndrome, living just for the sake of a man, his home, however much I love him. I'm just not the stay-at-home type. I'm me, an individual. My career means as much to me as any man's . . .'

His reply astounded her.

'What's so particularly feminine about staying at home? Successful women have just as much appeal. There's no reason why a man and a woman shouldn't love deeply yet still be enormous successes in their own right. You're certainly very different to all the other women I've met. How come you've never found a man to appreciate you . . . your particular talents?'

Did that mean *he* appreciated them? Her heart beat a little faster.

'Because all the men I've ever met have disapproved of career women; they've been looking for cosy, domesticated "pets" to cook their meals and raise their children.'

'Children!' She thought his face darkened. 'How do *you* feel about children, Josslyn?'

She hesitated. They seemed, in the latter part of their discussion, to have grown closer together. It had actually begun to seem possible that she and Juan were suited, by mental inclination as well as physical. But was *this* the final test? Coming of a family with such strong dynastic feelings, Juan might want children, whereas she ... Should she be honest, or pretend a maternal inclination she did not feel? No. Honesty was essential, even if it meant losing everything on one throw.

'I like children,' she said carefully, 'other people's children I mean. I'm not unnatural enough to dislike them. But ... but I don't want any of my own.' She tensed, waiting for his reaction.

'Neither do I.'

'You ... you don't?'

'No. I intend to go on with my work among the Indians ... it means being away from home for long stretches. I'd like my wife to be with me, at least some of the time, but no children. It's no, life for a child ... and I won't risk passing on this accursed birthmark, passing on the burden *I've* had to bear.'

Josslyn bent her head in thought. It seemed that in most things they were entirely in accord ... but for one thing. Nowhere in their conversation had love been mentioned. Juan had wanted her enough to marry her ... and she knew marriage for him was no light commitment. His religion forbade divorce. *She* loved *him*. Was that enough?'

'Well, Josslyn, which is it to be? A barren existence apart ... or a full, fulfilled life together?' He was not touching her, deliberately letting her make up her mind without physical coercion of any kind.

On the instant her mind was made up and she turned to tell him so, a light in her eyes that, unknowingly, revealed much to him. But before she could speak there was a soft, surreptitious knock at the door.

'Damn! Who's that? Don't answer it!' Juan commanded.

But in his absorption with the subject that obsessed him, Juan had omitted to lock the door. It swung open now and Daphne Ransome appeared, her expression

anxious, questioning, Harry Livings upon her heels.
Daphne clapped a hand to her mouth.

'Oh! I ... that is ... we thought you might be alone
by now ...' Her eyes took in the fact that they were
both still fully dressed and her features relaxed a little.
'You must have had quite a lot to discuss?'

'We did.' Juan said grimly. 'We still have, isn't that
so, Josslyn?' He took her hand, the contact of their
flesh somehow becoming a kind of preliminary to the
more intimate caresses she knew he longed to initiate.
Much as she loved her mother and Harry, she could
have wished them anywhere else at this moment.

'Yes.' She blushed as she spoke. If only Daphne and
Harry had not chosen this particular moment to
intervene. She and Juan had been, she felt, upon the
verge of a greater, more significant understanding.

'Well!' Daphne looked doubtfully from one to the
other. 'If you're quite sure everything's all right?'

'Quite all right, Mother,' Josslyn said, with all the
new found confidence she felt.

'Then ... then I suppose we'd better leave you to
your discussion. We only wanted to tell you ...' she
hesitated, her cheeks turning a fiery red, 'that Harry
and I have decided ... that is ... Harry has asked me
to marry him!'

'Oh, Mother.' Her own preoccupations temporarily
forgotten, Josslyn jumped up to embrace first Daphne,
then Harry. 'Oh, I'm so happy for you.'

'You ... you don't mind?' Her mother enquired
anxiously. 'You don't think it's too soon after ... You
don't resent it, on your father's account? You were *so*
close,' she said wistfully, and Josslyn suddenly realised
the fact that Daphne had recognised a different kind of
closeness between father and daughter, closer in its way,
because of their shared interest, than between husband
and wife.

'If I know Dad, he'd want you to be happy!' Josslyn
said firmly.

'May I add *my* congratulations?' Juan had risen and came over to shake Harry's hand, to kiss Daphne's cheek. 'And wish you all the happiness we hope to enjoy ourselves.' He placed his arm around Josslyn's waist.

'*You're* going to be married, too?' Daphne asked incredulously, joyfully.

'We already *are* married, Mother,' Josslyn put in, before Juan could speak, and knew the reward for her expression of trust in the convulsive tightening of his clasp, heard his swift intake of breath.

There were more kisses and congratulations before Daphne and Harry departed in a flurry of apologies for having disturbed them. Suddenly shy now after her brief spurt of courage, Josslyn found herself unable to meet Juan's eyes as he drew her towards the bed.

'Just one more thing,' he said shortly, 'before . . .' He delved into the pocket of the jacket he had discarded and brought out a small box.

Wonderingly, Josslyn opened it. Within lay two rings, one a plain gold band, the other bearing a green stone with a deeply carved design. She looked up at him questioningly.

'Is this . . .'

'Yes. I had it made from the piece of green jadeite you found in the ruins. Remember?'

How could she forget any detail of her life since she'd met him? But the design? She wasn't sure she liked it. The craftsmanship was perfect. Much skill had been needed to incise the forms . . . an eagle and a serpent. The serpent's coils were wound around the bird . . . a bird that did not struggle, but seemed to enfold the snake in curved, loving wings.

'They represent us,' he murmured huskily, 'mutually dangerous, but eternally linked.' He slid the rings on to her third finger. 'Now everyone will know you're mine . . . and you *will* come back to Mexico, Josslyn?'

'I want to,' she murmured, then, more strongly, 'I want to help you with your work . . .'

'We'll work together,' he assured her. 'Our skills shall be complementary, as we are to each other . . .'

Longing stirred and she went willingly into his arms; longing and with it the surging, primitive awareness of being female. He had still not mentioned love but . . .'

'Josslyn, just one more thing. About my grandmother . . .'

'Hush!' She laid a finger on his lips. Poor, deluded woman she thought, her only crime in reality was ignorance. 'I've forgiven her . . .'

'And me?' he murmured against the forbidding finger.

'You?' Aware of her power over him, she could not resist teasing him a little, punishing him. She hesitated.

'Yes?' His voice was deep, edged with anxiety.

'There's nothing to forgive,' she whispered, offering her lips. 'I understand everything.'

'Josslyn,' he murmured moments later. '*Te quiero mucho*. I love you.'

'You . . . love . . . me?' she whispered incredulously. '*Really* love me . . . not just . . .'

'*Verdad, verdad!* Really, really!'

She had to believe in the intensity with which he uttered the words.

'Something I never thought to feel for any woman. Not just this physical attraction, but something much deeper . . . And you? You still . . .'

'I've never stopped loving you,' she told him, 'even when I tried to tell myself that I hated you. I knew nothing could ever kill my love. Oh, Juan. I love you, I want you . . .'

Again his mouth silenced hers; and there was no more talking, only loving as she had dreamt it would be . . . as it would be from that moment on.

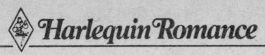
Harlequin Romance

Coming Next Month

2785 SOME SAY LOVE Lindsay Armstrong
Rescuing his late friend's daughter becomes habit-forming for
an Australian real-estate tycoon. So when she recklessly falls in
love with him, he marries her. But does he love her?

2786 PRISONER OF SHADOW MOUNTAIN
      Mariel Kirk
When a successful model regains consciousness after a plane
crash her mind is blank. She knows only that she's attracted to
her ruggedly handsome rescuer—despite the wedding band
found in her belongings!

2787 A GIRL NAMED ROSE Betty Neels
Quite by accident, a vacationing English staff nurse encounters
an impressive Dutch surgeon. And quite by surprise, she's
chosen to work with him, though he probably would have
preferred her pretty friend.

2788 HEARTBREAK PLAINS Valerie Parv
Australia's Chedoona Downs is a beautiful place to stay—even
as a virtual prisoner. But once her rich and powerful captor
discovers she's not the woman he's looking for, why won't he
let her go?

2789 MISLEADING ENCOUNTER Jessica Steele
When it's time to fall in love, a London model decides to
choose carefully. And the aggressive electronics company
owner love chooses for her doesn't seem a good choice at all.

2790 SWEET POISON Angela Wells
To conceal her sister's extramarital tryst, a young woman new
to Spain accepts dishonor—never dreaming she'll be forced
to marry the one man capable of exposing her lie...and
her innocence.

Available in September wherever paperback books are sold,
or through Harlequin Reader Service.

In the U.S.   In Canada
P.O. Box 1397   P.O. Box 2800, Postal Station A
Buffalo, N.Y.   5170 Yonge Street
14240-1397   Willowdale, Ontario M2N 6J3

A terrible family secret drives Kristi Johannssen to California, where she finds glamor, romance and...a threat to her life!

BEYOND THE RAINBOW

MARGARET CHITTENDEN

Power and elegance, jealousy and deceit, even murder, stoke fires of passion in this glittering novel set in the fashion world of Hollywood, on the dazzling coast of Southern California.

Take 4 books & a surprise gift FREE

SPECIAL LIMITED-TIME OFFER

Mail to   **Harlequin Reader Service®**

In the U.S.	In Canada
901 Fuhrmann Blvd.	P.O. Box 2800, Station "A"
P.O. Box 1394	5170 Yonge Street
Buffalo, N.Y. 14240-1394	Willowdale, Ontario M2N 6J3

YES! Please send me 4 free Harlequin Presents® novels and my free surprise gift. Then send me 8 brand-new novels every month as they come off the presses. Bill me at the low price of $1.75 each ($1.95 in Canada)—a 11% saving off the retail price. There are no shipping, handling or other hidden costs. There is no minimum number of books I must purchase. I can always return a shipment and cancel at any time. Even if I never buy another book from Harlequin, the 4 free novels and the surprise gift are mine to keep forever.

116-BPR-BP6F

Name   (PLEASE PRINT)

Address   Apt. No.

City   State/Prov.   Zip/Postal Code

ATTRACTIVE, SPACE SAVING BOOK RACK

Display your most prized novels on this handsome and sturdy book rack. The hand-rubbed walnut finish will blend into your library decor with quiet elegance, providing a practical organizer for your favorite hard-or soft-covered books.

Only $9.95

**Approximately
16" x 8"
when assembled**

Assembles in seconds!

To order, rush your name, address and zip code, along with a check or money order for $10.70 ($9.95 plus 75¢ postage and handling) (New York residents add appropriate sales tax), payable to *Harlequin Reader Service* to:

In the U.S.

Harlequin Reader Service
Book Rack Offer
901 Fuhrmann Blvd.
P.O. Box 1325
Buffalo, NY 14269-1325

Offer not available in Canada.

BKR-1